Here's what teens are saying about Bluford High:

"As soon as I finished one book, I couldn't wait to start the next one. No books have ever made me do that before."
—*Terrance W.*

"The suspense got to be so great I could feel the blood pounding in my ears."
—*Yolanda F*

"Once I started reading them, I just couldn't stop, not even to go to sleep."
—*Brian M.*

"Great books! I hope they write more."
—*Eric J.*

"When I finished these books, I went back to the beginning and read them all over again. That's how much I loved them."
—*Caren B.*

"I found it very easy to lose myself in these books. They kept my interest from beginning to end and were always realistic. The characters are vivid, and the endings left me in eager anticipation of the next book."
—*Keziah J.*

Lost and Found

ANNE SCHRAFF

Series Editor: Paul Langan

SCHOLASTIC INC.
New York Toronto London Auckland Sydney
Mexico City New Delhi Hong Kong Buenos Aires

ISBN-13: 978-0-439-89839-3
ISBN-10: 0-439-89839-0

12 11 10 9   10 11 12/0

Printed in the U.S.A.   01

This edition first printing, January 2007

Chapter 1

Darcy Wills winced at the loud rap music coming from her sister's room.

My rhymes were rockin'
MC's were droppin'
People shoutin' and hip-hoppin'
Step to me and you'll be inferior
'Cause I'm your lyrical superior.

Darcy went to Grandma's room. The darkened room smelled of lilac perfume, Grandma's favorite, but since her stroke Grandma did not notice it, or much of anything.

"Bye, Grandma," Darcy whispered from the doorway. "I'm going to school now."

Just then, the music from Jamee's room cut off, and Jamee rushed into the hallway.

"Like she even hears you," Jamee said as she passed Darcy. Just two years younger than Darcy, Jamee was in eighth grade, though she looked older.

"It's still nice to talk to her. Sometimes she understands. You want to pretend she's not here or something?"

"She's not," Jamee said, grabbing her backpack.

"Did you study for your math test?" Darcy asked. Mom was an emergency-room nurse who worked rotating shifts. Most of the time, Mom was too tired to pay much attention to the girls' schoolwork. So Darcy tried to keep track of Jamee.

"Mind your own business," Jamee snapped.

"You got two D's on your last report card," Darcy scolded. "You wanna flunk?" Darcy did not want to sound like a nagging parent, but Jamee wasn't doing her best. Maybe she couldn't make A's like Darcy, but she could do better.

Jamee stomped out of the apartment, slamming the door behind her. "Mom's trying to get some rest!" Darcy yelled. "Do you have to be so selfish?" But Jamee was already gone, and the apartment was suddenly quiet.

Darcy loved her sister. Once, they had been good friends. But now all Jamee cared about was her new group of rowdy friends. They leaned on cars outside of school and turned up rap music on their boom boxes until the street seemed to tremble like an earthquake. Jamee had even stopped hanging out with her old friend Alisha Wrobel, something she used to do every weekend.

Darcy went back into the living room, where her mother sat in the recliner sipping coffee. "I'll be home at 2:30, Mom," Darcy said. Mom smiled faintly. She was tired, always tired. And lately she was worried too. The hospital where she worked was cutting staff. It seemed each day fewer people were expected to do more work. It was like trying to climb a mountain that keeps getting taller as you go. Mom was forty-four, but just yesterday she said, *"I'm like an old car that's run out of warranty, baby. You know what happens then. Old car is ready for the junk heap. Well, maybe that hospital is gonna tell me one of these days—'Mattie Mae Wills, we don't need you anymore. We can get somebody younger and cheaper.'"*

"Mom, you're not old at all," Darcy had said, but they were only words, empty words. They could not erase the dark, weary lines from beneath her mother's eyes.

Darcy headed down the street toward Bluford High School. It was not a terrible neighborhood they lived in; it just was not good. Many front yards were not cared for. Debris—fast food wrappers, plastic bags, old newspapers—blew around and piled against fences and curbs. Darcy hated that. Sometimes she and other kids from school spent Saturday mornings cleaning up, but it seemed a losing battle. Now, as she walked, she tried to focus on small spots of beauty along the way. Mrs. Walker's pink and white roses bobbed proudly in the morning breeze. The Hustons' rock garden was carefully designed around a wooden windmill.

As she neared Bluford, Darcy thought about the science project that her biology teacher, Ms. Reed, was assigning. Darcy was doing hers on tidal pools. She was looking forward to visiting a real tidal pool, taking pictures, and doing research. Today, Ms. Reed would

4

be dividing the students into teams of two. Darcy wanted to be paired with her close friend, Brisana Meeks. They were both excellent students, a cut above most kids at Bluford, Darcy thought.

"Today, we are forming project teams so that each student can gain something valuable from the other," Ms. Reed said as Darcy sat at her desk. Ms. Reed was a tall, stately woman who reminded Darcy of the Statue of Liberty. She would have been a perfect model for the statue if Lady Liberty had been a black woman. She never would have been called pretty, but it was possible she might have been called a handsome woman. "For this assignment, each of you will be working with someone you've never worked with before."

Darcy was worried. If she was not teamed with Brisana, maybe she would be teamed with some really dumb student who would pull her down. Darcy was a little ashamed of herself for thinking that way. Grandma used to say that all flowers are equal, but different. The simple daisy was just as lovely as the prize rose. But still Darcy did not want to be paired with some weak partner who would lower her grade.

"Darcy Wills will be teamed with Tarah Carson," Ms. Reed announced.

Darcy gasped. Not Tarah! Not that big, chunky girl with the brassy voice who squeezed herself into tight skirts and wore lime green or hot pink satin tops and cheap jewelry. Not Tarah who hung out with Cooper Hodden, that loser who was barely hanging on to his football eligibility. Darcy had heard that Cooper had been left back once or twice and even got his driver's license as a sophomore. Darcy's face felt hot with anger. Why was Ms. Reed doing this?

Hakeem Randall, a handsome, shy boy who sat in the back row, was teamed with the class blabbermouth, LaShawn Appleby. Darcy had a secret crush on Hakeem since freshman year. So far she had only shared this with her diary, never with another living soul.

It was almost as though Ms. Reed was playing some devilish game. Darcy glanced at Tarah, who was smiling broadly. Tarah had an enormous smile, and her teeth contrasted harshly with her dark red lipstick. "Great," Darcy muttered under her breath.

Ms. Reed ordered the teams to meet so they could begin to plan their projects.

As she sat down by Tarah, Darcy was instantly sickened by a syrupy-sweet odor. *She must have doused herself with cheap perfume this morning,* Darcy thought.

"Hey, girl," Tarah said. "Well, don't you look down in the mouth. What's got you lookin' that way?"

It was hard for Darcy to meet new people, especially someone like Tarah, a person Aunt Charlotte would call "low class." These were people who were loud and rude. They drank too much, used drugs, got into fights and ruined the neighborhood. They yelled ugly insults at people, even at their friends. Darcy did not actually know that Tarah did anything like this personally, but she seemed like the type who did.

"I just didn't think you'd be interested in tidal pools," Darcy explained.

Tarah slammed her big hand on the desk, making her gold bracelets jangle like ice cubes in a glass, and laughed. Darcy had never heard a mule bray, but she was sure it made exactly the same sound. Then Tarah leaned close and whispered, "Girl, I don't know a tidal pool from a fool. Ms. Reed stuck us together to mess with our heads, you hear what I'm sayin'?"

"Maybe we could switch to other partners," Darcy said nervously.

A big smile spread slowly over Tarah's face. "Nah, I think I'm gonna enjoy this. You're always sittin' here like a princess collecting your A's. Now you gotta work with a regular person, so you better loosen up, girl!"

Darcy felt as if her teeth were glued to her tongue. She fumbled in her bag for her outline of the project. It all seemed like a horrible joke now. She and Tarah Carson standing knee-deep in the muck of a tidal pool!

"Worms live there, don't they?" Tarah asked, twisting a big gold ring on her chubby finger.

"Yeah, I guess," Darcy replied.

"Big green worms," Tarah continued. "So if you get your feet stuck in the bottom of that old tidal pool, and you can't get out, do the worms crawl up your clothes?"

Darcy ignored the remark. "I'd like for us to go there soon, you know, look around."

"My boyfriend, Cooper, he goes down to the ocean all the time. He can take us. He says he's seen these fiddler crabs. They look like big spiders, and they'll try to bite your toes off. Cooper says so," Tarah said.

"Stop being silly," Darcy shot back. "If you're not even going to be serious . . . "

"You think you're better than me, don't you?" Tarah suddenly growled.

"I never said—" Darcy blurted.

"You don't have to say it, girl. It's in your eyes. You think I'm a low-life and you're something special. Well, I got more friends than you got fingers and toes together. You got no friends, and everybody laughs at you behind your back. Know what the word on you is? Darcy Wills give you the chills."

Just then, the bell rang, and Darcy was glad for the excuse to turn away from Tarah, to hide the hot tears welling in her eyes. She quickly rushed from the classroom, relieved that school was over. Darcy did not think she could bear to sit through another class just now.

Darcy headed down the long street towards home. She did not like Tarah. Maybe it was wrong, but it was true. Still, Tarah's brutal words hurt. Even stupid, awful people might tell you the truth about yourself. And Darcy did not have any real friends, except for Brisana. Maybe the other kids were mocking her behind her back. Darcy was very slender, not as shapely as many of the other girls. She remembered the time when Cooper Hodden was hanging in front of the deli with his friends, and he yelled as Darcy went by, *"Hey, is that really a female there? Sure don't look like it. Looks more like an old broomstick with hair."* His companions laughed rudely, and Darcy had walked a little faster.

A terrible thought clawed at Darcy. Maybe *she* was the loser, not Tarah. Tarah was always hanging with a bunch of kids, laughing and joking. She would go down the hall to the lockers and greetings would come from everywhere. "Hey, Tarah!" "What's up, Tar?" "See ya at lunch, girl." When Darcy went to the lockers, there was dead silence.

Darcy usually glanced into stores on her way home from school. She enjoyed looking at the trays of chicken feet and pork ears at the little Asian grocery store. Sometimes she would even steal a glance at the diners sitting by the picture window at the Golden Grill Restaurant. But today she stared straight ahead, her shoulders drooping.

If this had happened last year, she would have gone directly to Grandma's house, a block from where Darcy lived. How many times had Darcy and Jamee run to Grandma's, eaten applesauce cookies, drunk cider, and poured out their troubles to Grandma. Somehow, their problems would always dissolve in the warmth of her love and wisdom. But now Grandma was a frail figure in the corner of their apartment, saying little. And what little she did say made less and less sense.

Darcy was usually the first one home. The minute she got there, Mom left for the hospital to take the 3:00 to 11:00 shift in the ER. By the time Mom finished her paperwork at the hospital, she would be lucky to be home again by midnight. After Mom left, Darcy went to Grandma's room to give her the malted nutrition drink that the doctor ordered her to have three times a day.

"Want to drink your chocolate malt, Grandma?" Darcy asked, pulling up a chair beside Grandma's bed.

Grandma was sitting up, and her eyes were open. "No. I'm not hungry," she said listlessly. She always said that.

"You need to drink your malt, Grandma," Darcy insisted, gently putting the straw between the pinched lips.

Grandma sucked the malt slowly. "Grandma, nobody likes me at school," Darcy said. She did not expect any response. But there was a strange comfort in telling Grandma anyway. "Everybody laughs at me. It's because I'm shy and maybe stuck-up, too, I guess. But I don't mean to be. Stuck-up, I mean. Maybe I'm weird. I could be weird, I guess. I could be like Aunt Charlotte . . ." Tears rolled down Darcy's cheeks. Her heart ached with loneliness. There was nobody to talk to anymore, nobody who had time to listen, nobody who understood.

Grandma blinked and pushed the straw away. Her eyes brightened as they did now and then. "You are a wonderful girl. Everybody knows that," Grandma said in an almost normal voice. It happened like that sometimes. It was like being in the middle of a dark storm and having the clouds part, revealing a patch of clear, sunlit blue. For just a few precious minutes, Grandma was bright-eyed and saying normal things.

"Oh, Grandma, I'm so lonely," Darcy cried, pressing her head against Grandma's small shoulder.

"You were such a beautiful baby," Grandma said, stroking her hair. "'That one is going to shine like the morning star.' That's what I told your Mama. 'That child is going to shine like the morning star.' Tell me, Angelcake, is your daddy home yet?"

Darcy straightened. "Not yet." Her heart pounded so hard, she could feel it thumping in her chest. Darcy's father had not been home in five years.

"Well, tell him to see me when he gets home. I want him to buy you that blue dress you liked in the store window. That's for you, Angelcake. Tell him I've got money. My social security came, you know. I have money for the blue dress," Grandma said, her eyes slipping shut.

Just then, Darcy heard the apartment door slam. Jamee had come home. Now she stood in the hall, her hands belligerently on her hips. "Are you talking to Grandma again?" Jamee demanded.

"She was talking like normal," Darcy said. "Sometimes she does. You know she does."

"That is so stupid," Jamee snapped. "She never says anything right anymore. Not anything!" Jamee's voice trembled.

Darcy got up quickly and set down the can of malted milk. She ran to Jamee and put her arms around her sister. "Jamee, I know you're hurting too."

"Oh, don't be stupid," Jamee protested, but Darcy hugged her more tightly, and in a few seconds Jamee was crying. "She was the best thing in this stupid house," Jamee cried. "Why'd she have to go?"

"She didn't go," Darcy said. "Not really."

"She did! She did!" Jamee sobbed. She struggled free of Darcy, ran to her room, and slammed the door. In a minute, Darcy heard the bone-rattling sound of rap music.

Chapter 2

"You still up?" Darcy's mother asked when she got home.

"I couldn't sleep," Darcy said.

Mom settled into her recliner. "I need to sit down and catch my breath, baby, before I shower and go to bed. What a night we had. Two boys in critical from drive-bys, a four-car accident on the freeway, a broken neck, plus the usual fevers and chest pains. And then we had a memo from our new administrator— seems like we're wasting money."

Darcy hoped she might get the chance to talk to her mother about the problems at school, and maybe about Jamee's attitude. Darcy went to get some hot chocolate for them, but by the time she returned, her mother was dozing. "Mom?" Darcy asked softly, but Mom's even breathing continued. She

15

was exhausted. Darcy did not have the heart to rouse her.

There was so much Darcy wanted to talk about. When Mom was sixteen, was she popular at school? What do you do when you're a loner and you cannot seem to break out of it? And Jamee. She was worried about Jamee. A few times Darcy saw her riding in a car with some boys from Bluford. Jamee was only in middle school. Those older guys scared Darcy—some were gangster wanna-be's. One of them, Bobby Wallace, had already been in trouble with the police for something or other. Once, last week, Darcy had tried to talk to her mother about Jamee, but Mom just said, *"Oh, she'll be okay. She's at that age when kids try to rebel and take things to the extreme. I was lucky with you, praise the Lord. You never went through that phase, Darcy. Your sister is a different story. Y'all have always been as different as night and day. But Jamee's a smart girl, and she'll come out of this phase pretty soon."*

Darcy drank down her hot chocolate and rinsed out the cups, then she headed for her room. She sat on the edge of her bed for a few minutes, staring at the photographs on her dresser. Mom, Grandma, her, and Jamee. There had been older family photographs with Dad included, but they were all hidden away somewhere. Darcy remembered the last photo taken with Dad. It showed eleven-year-old Darcy in braids and blue ribbons, wearing a lovely blue dress with a lacy collar, and Jamee, nine, her big brown eyes bright with mischief. That was taken a few months before Dad left.

It had been harder on Jamee than on Darcy when Dad left. Darcy was closer to Mom, but Jamee was Daddy's little girl. They went to basketball games together and just seemed to have a companionship that Darcy never had with her father. On a family hike in the Laguna Mountains, Jamee and her father chose a special tree, a giant cedar. One day they stood by their tree, and Dad dubbed Jamee "Princess of the World," surprising her with a tiny crown for her head. Jamee's squeals of joy had echoed through the forest that day.

"Why did Daddy leave us?" Jamee had demanded tearfully when it was clear he would not be coming home.

"Leaving was more fun than staying," Mom had answered bitterly.

Darcy always suspected her mother had seen some warning signs, but to Darcy and Jamee it had been a complete shock. Jamee made up stories for a long time after, trying to explain why her father had left. She had shared them with Darcy. Daddy had a terrible disease, and he did not want to burden his family with it. He had some secret government job that was so dangerous he could not risk being around his family anymore. But, eventually, even Jamee had laughed at her own fantasies. She had grudgingly accepted her mother's simple explanation—Daddy had found something else that meant more to him than his family. Darcy remembered it was about then that Jamee slowly began to change, to have angry, sad moods, to be cynical.

Darcy went to bed, but she did not sleep for a while. She relived her last meeting with her father, when he took her and Jamee for ice cream on a hot August afternoon. Darcy later figured it was the best way he could manage to say goodbye. Darcy and Jamee were just little girls, so they did not question his heavy step, the way his jaw was set. They were too busy deciding between chocolate chip and strawberry ice cream to pay

attention to his odd mumbling. *"Nothin'
ever happens around here, except I'm getting older."* He talked about being a
teenager in New York and what a happening place it was, about the jazz clubs,
and dancing until dawn. *"Man grows old
too fast around here,"* he said. *"Gets dead
before they put him in the box."*

The day Dad left, he kissed Darcy,
then kissed and hugged Jamee so hard
that she giggled and protested. After
putting the girls on a trolley home, he had
turned and walked away faster than
Darcy had ever seen him walk before.
Darcy did not think about it then, but
now she figured he walked so quickly
because he knew what he was doing was
wrong. The faster he walked away, the
sooner he could escape the truth—that he
was abandoning his wife and daughters.

Darcy forced herself to stop remembering and finally fell asleep. In the
morning, she dreaded the thought of
going to school and seeing Tarah. Darcy
pondered different ways of handling the
problem. Finally, when she walked into
class, she just sat beside Tarah and said
briskly, "Hi. You said your boyfriend
could drive us to the tidal pool. When
could he do that?"

Tarah was sketching in her note-book. To Darcy's surprise, she was drawing pretty horses prancing across the pages. "Saturday afternoon," Tarah said, without looking up.

"That'd be good," Darcy replied, still staring at the sketches. "I didn't know you drew stuff."

"I do lots of things you don't know about," Tarah said in a testy voice.

"Those are good drawings," Darcy said.

"Why you bein' so nice, girl?" Tarah demanded.

"I'm not. I just—"

"My Mama says when folks who used to look down their noses at you start bein' nice, look out! They butter you up, then they stick you in the oven!" Tarah said.

"That's the kind of thing my Aunt Charlotte would say," Darcy blurted out. "She's suspicious of everybody. She has a good job and she's saving her money and she means to be the only one spending any. And she lives alone to make sure of that."

Tarah was silent for a moment, as if she was surprised at how honest Darcy was being. "I wouldn't want to live by myself," she said. "It'd be too lonely."

"My grandma is the opposite of Aunt Charlotte. She says it's worth it to have friends even if once in a while somebody does you wrong. She says love is worth it, even when it hurts." Darcy could not believe she was sharing something so personal with Tarah. She had never shared family stuff with anyone—not even Brisana.

For lunch that day, Darcy and Brisana met at their usual spot. They liked it under an oak tree where it was shady and secluded. "Poor Darcy," Brisana said as she pried open her container of yogurt. "How can you stand working with that dumb fat girl?"

Darcy wished Brisana would not make fun of Tarah, but she kept her thoughts to herself. "I'm making the best of it."

"Ms. Reed stuck me with Lori Samson. What a fool! And she has that terrible case of zits too! I think Ms. Reed resents pretty girls because she's so plain-looking. Can you imagine what she looked like when she was a teenager?" Brisana rocked back laughing.

."Cooper Hodden is driving me and Tarah to the tidal pool on Saturday," Darcy said.

"Oh Darcy! You're riding with that loser?" Brisana cried, almost dropping her yogurt. "I'd never ride with him. I mean, Cooper is just the kind of fool who would date somebody like Tarah Carson!"

Darcy munched on her apple. Brisana rarely had anything nice to say about anybody. Darcy remembered sitting with her many times while both of them talked bad about other kids. That girl dressed like she wore clothes from a thrift store, and that boy's breath smelled of garlic, and what stupid answers they gave in class! It seemed fun at the time, but now Darcy wondered if that was what she really wanted to do anymore, day after day.

Brisana leaned back in the grass, smiling. "Guess what? Hakeem Randall thinks he's got a shot at being valedictorian in two years. Hakeem! He stutters, for crying out loud!"

"Only when he's really nervous," Darcy said in a small voice. She had never told Brisana about her crush on Hakeem. He was bright, cute, and sweet, but very, very shy.

"Yeah, right, can you just imagine how much that boy would stutter if he was valedictorian?" Brisana laughed.

"He'd just stand there looking stupid because he'd be so nervous. Everybody'd look at him and say, 'What a fool!'"

Darcy glanced at her watch. "Oh, I gotta get some books from the library before next period," she said.

"See you later, Darcy. And good luck with the pig-girl," Brisana said, gathering her books.

Darcy wanted to say, *"Please don't call her that. It really bothers me when you call her that. I mean, I don't like her or anything, but just don't call her a pig-girl."* But Darcy instead said, "Yeah, see you later."

Darcy was in the school library searching for books on tidal pools when she heard a familiar voice. Bobby Wallace was with a friend on the other side of the bookshelves. Darcy drew closer without the boys seeing her.

"How you get hold of that CD, man?" the other boy asked Bobby.

"I got me a girl who'll do anything for me, you hear what I'm sayin'? She in the store and I say, 'Grab me that,' and she will, 'cause she do anything I ask, see? She crazy 'bout me, you hear me?" Bobby boasted.

"Don't she get caught or nothing?" the other boy asked.

"No, man, she smooth. Besides, that fool so busy with another customer he don't see nothin'. I pipe the tune and she dances, you hear what I'm sayin'?" Bobby bragged. "She only fourteen, but, man, she look so good everybody think she eighteen."

Darcy felt as if a bolt of electricity had gone through her. Was Bobby talking about Jamee? He had to be! She was the only middle-school girl Darcy ever saw hanging with Bobby and his friends. There was always loud music blasting from Bobby's car and guys leaning out picking on kids they would spot on the sidewalk. Jamee was vulnerable. After all, Bobby was good-looking and older, and she had to be the girl dancing to the tune he was piping, stealing for him. That was bad enough, but how soon would it be before she was in the car during a drive-by shooting or something? Last year a pair of older kids convinced a fifteen-year-old girl to shoot another driver as part of a gang initiation. Now she was facing a murder charge as an adult.

When Darcy got home from school, she fed Grandma her pudding and then waited for Jamee. Darcy could not even open her books and start her homework until she talked to her sister. Mom had to rush to the hospital to make a staff meeting before her shift began. Everybody at the hospital was jittery about new cutbacks ever since the hospital had hired a new administrator who promised to raise profits. Alone in the apartment, Darcy looked out the window and waited for her sister.

Jamee was late. Finally, an hour later than usual, Bobby Wallace dropped her off in his red Nissan. When Jamee came into the apartment, Darcy confronted her. "What are you doing hanging out with those people? They're too old for you. You're only in middle school—stick with kids your own age, not punks from Bluford!"

Jamee threw down her backpack and glared at Darcy. "They're not punks! They're my friends. The kids at middle school are stupid!"

"Bobby Wallace is trouble," Darcy snapped.

"He is not!" Jamee almost screamed.

"Jamee! Be quiet or you'll wake up Grandma!" Darcy warned.

"Who cares?" Jamee shouted all the louder. "She doesn't know if she's awake or sleeping anyway. And you don't know anything about Bobby Wallace. Everybody likes him, and there are girls who'd die for a chance to be in my shoes with Bobby. But he likes me best, and you're just jealous 'cause you're a sophomore in high school and you don't even have a boyfriend! You need to get a life and leave me alone."

Darcy felt the blood rushing to her face. She was handling this all wrong. Instead of helping Jamee, she was making her angry—which would drive her even closer to Bobby. Forcing her anger away, Darcy took a deep breath and stared at her sister. "Jamee, are you stealing stuff for Bobby?" Darcy demanded.

"Stealing?" Jamee repeated in a high-pitched tone. Darcy could always tell when Jamee was lying. Her voice went up an octave and trembled. "Why would I do that? Who said such a stupid thing?"

"Bobby was telling his friend at school today that he had you wrapped around his finger and you stole for him. He was laughing about it, and the other guy was laughing too. Bobby said you were just a stupid little kid and it was fun to make you dance to his tune." Darcy changed what Bobby had said a little, but she kept the main point. She felt bad for hurting Jamee, but she had to do it to help her sister.

Jamee stood there, a strange, terrible look on her face, as if her heart had stopped. She turned ashen. "Y-you're lying! Lying! Bobby wouldn't have said those things. He likes me. He l-loves me!"

Darcy was absolutely sure now that Jamee was the girl Bobby was talking about. "Do you want to get in trouble and go to jail because of some lousy punk who'd just as soon diss you as kiss you? Jamee, you should have heard them laughing about that CD you stole, about how stupid you were. Bobby said you'd do anything for him because you're a puppet on a string," Darcy said.

Jamee clamped her hands over her ears and screamed, "Stop it! I hate you, I hate you!" She turned and ran into her room, slamming the door so forcefully that the apartment walls shook. In a second's time, loud rap music thumped through the apartment.

And it's you I blame,
For makin' this noise,
For causin' this pain,
For takin' my voice.
And I need it to stop,
Like a tired old clock,
Before my body drops,
And my mind pops.

Darcy stood outside the closed door of her sister's room. Mingled with the blasts of furious music were other sounds—loud sobs, things striking the walls, the sound of shattering glass.

Chapter 3

"Who's that crying? Oh my Lord! Who's that crying?" Grandma moaned. Darcy rushed to Grandma's room. She was trying to get out of bed by herself. "One of the babies is crying, child!"

"No, no, Grandma," Darcy said. "Let me bring your walker. Here—I'll help you." Darcy wheeled the walker over to the side of the bed and slid her hand under Grandma's arm. "There we go."

"Who's that crying? Mattie Mae? Is that Mattie Mae bawling like that? Is that you crying, Charlotte? One of my babies is crying!" Grandma wailed. Mattie Mae and Charlotte were Grandma's daughters. Sometimes she thought they were children again.

"Grandma, everything is all right," Darcy said. "Do you want to go to the bathroom? I'll help you. Look, here's the walker."

Grandma's frail, veined hand grasped the walker as Darcy led her to the bathroom. Darcy remembered being a little girl and Grandma guiding the handlebars of her first bicycle. Grandma was vigorous then. She was strong and full of life until that stroke a year ago.

Darcy got Grandma back to bed and sat in the rocking chair next to her until she fell asleep. Sometimes Mom and Darcy moved the rocker to the living room so Grandma could be with them. But it was hard for her to sit up for long. On good days, she sat there and rocked and looked out into the small garden in the window box. Sometimes Grandma would remember the names of her favorite flowers: black and yellow pansies and bright blue lobelias. Sometimes she would recall planting them in the window box, and other times she would say her own mother had planted them. Now, with dwindling white hair like sparse cotton on her dark scalp, she lay on her pillow, her brown eyes opening again, looking alert.

"Angelcake, you're so good to me," Grandma declared, smiling. When she smiled, she almost looked as she had years earlier. Darcy had seen photographs of her grandmother when she was young. She was a beautiful, brown-eyed girl with thick, braided hair and a sweet little mouth. Now, smiling at Darcy, she did not look more than sixty, though she was seventy-seven.

"Grandma, I love you," Darcy said.

"Angelcake, your Daddy has to take you girls hiking again. Maybe tomorrow. When he comes home, we must tell him it's time to go hiking," Grandma said.

In the summer, before Dad left, the whole family would go hiking in the Laguna Mountains—not an exhausting hike, just one long enough to be fun. Mom would pack a lunch and leave it in the car. At the end of a hike, they would return to the same spot each time, and the girls would pounce on the mouth-watering goodies: crispy fried chicken, potato salad, iced tea, juicy peaches, and the best treat of all, Grandma's sweet potato pie. When there was a full moon, the Willses and Grandma would sometimes drive up at night. They would *ooh* and *ahh* over the moon, and Dad would point out constellations to Darcy and Jamee—the Big Dipper, Cassiopeia, the Seven Sisters, Orion. Then Mom would tell scary ghost stories right before it was time to head home. She was so good at telling them. Her favorite was called "The Tale of the Moon Monster." As the girls stared up at the full moon, so clear and bright you could see the dark shadows of the mountains, Mom would spin the creepy tale.

"Your mother has to tell her ghost stories," Grandma said, remembering too. "I told her ghost stories when she was little. Now she has to tell them to you."

"I remember, Grandma," Darcy said, overjoyed that for these brief moments, Grandma was almost normal.

"The Moon Monster," Grandma said, "how it crawls from the moon trailing silk clouds and comes down to the woods and captures people to take back to the moon because it's so lonely. Oh Lord, how my Mama scared me and my sisters with that story! And I told it to Mattie Mae and Charlotte and my boys." Grandma leaned forward a little and looked around, a puzzled expression on her face. "Is Mattie Mae home yet? And Charlotte? Tell those girls to get in and stop rollerskating on the sidewalk. It's almost dark now, and I want those girls to come inside."

"Yes, Grandma," Darcy said, holding Grandma's hand until she fell asleep again. A tear slipped down Darcy's cheek and left a salty trail across her lips. She mourned for what she had already lost of Grandma. The doctors did not know how long Grandma would live, but the grieving had already begun.

In the morning, Jamee ate her breakfast in sullen silence. Mom was still sleeping, but even if she had been at the breakfast table, she probably would not have noticed Jamee's attitude. Mom was too bone-tired and too nervous about the new hospital administrator to think of much else.

"I'm sorry about last night," Darcy said. "I didn't mean to yell at you."

Jamee forked scrambled eggs into her mouth and gulped her orange juice. She got up and said in a flat voice, "It doesn't matter. I mean, what do I care what Bobby Wallace says about me? Like I care what that stupid fool is saying. I don't even notice him anymore. I don't care about any guy. I hate them all."

"Some guys are nice," Darcy said.

"How would *you* know, Darcy?" Jamee asked.

"I know some nice guys at school, even if I don't date them. Guys like Hakeem Randall. He's always helping out with food drives and cleanup campaigns and stuff," Darcy replied.

"*Nice* is such a stupid word," Jamee said, strapping on her backpack and heading out the door.

Darcy did not want to spy on her sister, but when Jamee was gone, Darcy looked in her room. She wanted to find out what the sound of shattering glass last night was all about.

Darcy refused to look in Jamee's dresser drawers, but she did look in the trash can, which was full to overflowing. Sheets of newspaper were wrapped around something bulky, and Darcy carefully unwrapped it. She found a framed photograph of Bobby Wallace. Scrawled on the bottom was "To my girl, Jamee, Your Bobby." The glass over the photo had been smashed into splinters. The photo itself was defaced by a black felt pen. There were discarded clippings from school newspapers describing Bobby's triumphs on the football field.

Jamee had carefully clipped out every story, however briefly Bobby was mentioned. Now she had torn the clippings into shreds.

Darcy returned everything to the trash can, wrapping the newspapers around the shattered picture as Jamee had done. Darcy felt guilty that she had poked around among Jamee's hurtful memories, though she felt relieved that Jamee had seemed to cut ties with Bobby. Poor Jamee. She was wounded by Dad's leaving, Grandma's drifting away—and now she was hurt again.

On Saturday afternoon, Cooper and Tarah picked up Darcy for the trip to the tidal pool. Cooper drove an old pickup truck with a camper shell on the back.

Darcy brought along a thick notebook and her camera. All the way to the tidal pool, Tarah and Cooper were exchanging good-natured insults, then roaring with laughter.

"Girl, you so fat, every time you leave the all-you-can-eat restaurant, they close down for a few weeks!" Cooper said, laughing at his own joke.

"Coop, you so dumb, you went to a movie and the man at the ticket window said 'Under seventeen not admitted,' so you went home and brought back sixteen of your friends," Tarah shot back. Rocking side to side with laughter, she almost squeezed Darcy right out the door. "Darcy, girl, Coop's the most stupid guy at Bluford," Tarah added. "He thinks the school was named Bluford because the guy who built it had a blue Ford!"

"So, Einstein," Cooper said, looking at Tarah, "who was the school named for?"

"A guy named Bluford, you dummy. Some famous old guy named Bluford," Tarah answered.

Cooper roared again with laughter. "See? She don't know from nothing who Bluford is. If you so smart, you ought to know who this Bluford dude was."

"I do know," Tarah said. "His name was Jim Bluford, and he was a great football player who won the Super Bowl five times in a row."

Darcy smiled. Tarah was faking, of course. She had no more idea than Cooper did who Bluford was.

"A football player?" Cooper bellowed. "What kind of crazy answer is that, girl? You must be trippin'! Nobody would

36

name a school after some jock! Not even after Michael Jordan. No way! Bluford has to be some big-time politician or something."

"Actually," Darcy said, "the school was named for Guion Bluford, the first African American to go up in space. He rode one of the space shuttles."

Tarah wrinkled her nose. "Get outta here! You so weird to know something like that, girl."

"They talk about it at school assemblies," Darcy explained.

"Like we listen during those boring assemblies about stuff that happened a hundred years ago," Tarah said.

"Bluford went into space in the 1980's," Darcy added.

"That's why no one likes you, girl," Tarah said. "You know too much."

"Maybe when we get to that tidal pool we ought to feed her to the sharks," Cooper said, laughing loudly.

"There are no sharks in tidal pools," Darcy said. "The water is very shallow. I mean, picture a shark in a wading pool, right?"

"Man, this girl is making me crazy," Cooper told Tarah. "Let's lose her. We could say it was an accident."

"You should be glad to learn something," Darcy retorted. "Do you want to be ignorant all your life?"

"What's that supposed to mean?" Cooper shot back angrily. "Just 'cause I been left back in school you think I'm gonna be ignorant all my life?" he charged.

"That's not what I meant at all." Darcy tried to explain but gave up, realizing what a dreadful mistake this outing was.

The three sat in silence until the pickup truck rattled to a stop at the end of a street. From there, a long twisting path led to the tidal pool. Darcy slung her camera over her back and followed the winding rocky path toward the ocean's edge. She was happy to be out of the truck.

"What's a tidal pool anyway?" Tarah asked in a bored voice.

"It's a pool for the tide," Cooper chuckled. "Like rich folks got pools and the tide's got a pool. You hear what I'm sayin'?"

"It's a place where the sea meets the land," Darcy said. "The tide goes in and out, so sometimes the water is very shallow and sometimes it's deeper. Different kinds of creatures live in the water at different levels."

"Maybe this would be a good place to push her in," Tarah said as they made their way past a treacherous spot on the trail. Below, the water rolled against the rocks, making a foamy mist.

"Nah," Cooper said. "You need her to get your project done. You gonna flunk biology as dumb as you are. Then you'll be stuck in high school for the rest of your natural life. This brainy girl is gonna get you outta high school before you got as many gray hairs as my granny."

"You really are hilarious, you two," Darcy said sarcastically. "You should have your own TV show."

When they finally reached the tidal pool, Cooper exclaimed, "Man, it's crawling with weird things. Look at all the stuff floating around. Too bad we didn't bring bottles to catch some of that stuff."

"We're not allowed to remove anything," Darcy warned. "That would spoil the ecosystem of the tidal pool. We can take lots of pictures, though."

"What's that green thing?" Tarah asked. "Ewwww, it's disgusting!"

"That's a sea cucumber," Darcy said.

"Looks like you, Coop," Tarah declared.

"Hey, babe, I see you right there! That thing wriggling under the water. Look at it, it's your spittin' image!" Cooper taunted.

"That's a sea urchin," Darcy said. She snapped some pictures of the tidal pool and began to write observations in her notebook. She already saw starfish and more sea urchins along with a lot of kelp and algae. Some of the rubbery kelp was lying on the rocks in small patches of sand.

Darcy was peering into the water, intent on observing a purple sun star, when she felt something large and wriggly drop down the back of her pullover sweater. "Cooper!" Darcy screamed as the laughing boy danced away in glee. Tarah was doubled over laughing too.

Darcy felt the creature scuttling along her back. Quickly she grabbed her sweater and began shaking it violently. "Get it out!" she screamed.

"It's only a leech," Tarah said, laughing wildly. "I mean, it's got a million legs and it sucks blood, but leeches gotta live too, girl."

"Whoa, look at that girl dance," Cooper said as Darcy frantically tried to shake the bug from her sweater. The black insect, a water bug, finally dropped to the sand and scurried away into the weeds. Furious, Darcy aimed a kick at Cooper's shins.

"Owww," he cried, stumbling backwards.

"I knew you were crude and stupid," Darcy screamed at the pair, "but I didn't think you were so childish that you'd do something like that!"

"It was a joke," Cooper said, rubbing his leg where Darcy had kicked him. "Girl, you got a mean hoof!"

"Can't you get off your high horse long enough to take a joke?" Tarah yelled, siding with Cooper. Darcy was not surprised by that. These two were cut from the same cloth, she thought.

Darcy felt angry and humiliated. "I'm telling Ms. Reed on Monday that I want another partner!"

"Good!" Tarah shot back. "I don't want to work with no stuck-up girl who thinks she's better than everyone else. You ain't no better than the rest of us."

Darcy shook with rage as she stuffed her notebook into her backpack. "I'll find another way home. I don't want to ride with you," she snapped.

"You ain't welcome to ride with us," Cooper shouted. "You prob'ly busted my leg!"

"Good!" Darcy shot back over her shoulder as she started up the path. "Next time you'll think twice before you play stupid pranks!"

Darcy was breathing hard when she reached the top of the hill where the street was. Her anger had cooled a little. Cooper's stunt was stupid, but he did not mean any real harm by it. It was just that he was seventeen going on five years old.

Darcy walked down the nearly deserted street to the bus stop. As she stood there waiting for the bus, Tarah and Cooper roared by in the pickup truck. They yelled something at her, but Darcy pretended not to hear.

Darcy dreaded the long bus trip home. By car, the trip took about twenty-five minutes. But by the time she changed buses, the trip home would take an hour and a half.

Darcy had been sitting on the bus bench for ten minutes when she noticed an old silver Toyota parked under a tree down the street. An overweight, middle-aged man wearing a New York Yankees baseball cap sat at the wheel. Darcy could not make out his face through the dirty front windshield. He seemed to be looking in her direction, but she could not be sure.

Darcy looked around nervously. She wished the bus would hurry up and come. There was no one else on the street, and it was getting darker as the sun slid behind the horizon. Darcy was not even sure what time the bus was supposed to come. Usually buses ran every thirty minutes, but maybe this was a less popular route and they did not run that often.

Glancing at the Toyota, Darcy was worried. *What if that guy gets out of his car and comes walking over? What if he's dangerous? What if he has a gun or a knife?*

Suddenly the door of the sedan opened. The driver swung a leg out. He was getting out of the car! Darcy looked around the empty street desperately. Maybe she should just take off running. But what if he chased her? What if he had a gun and shot at her while she ran? She could not outrun a bullet!

Chapter 4

Darcy was about to sprint away when she saw the bus lumber into view. "Thank goodness," Darcy sighed. The bus would be here in seconds. The man in the Toyota seemed to figure that out too. He got back in the car and slammed the door. He started the Toyota and made a U-turn in the street just as the bus doors opened. Darcy scrambled into the bus and slid her dollar bills into the fare box beside the driver. The driver gave her a transfer pass that almost fell from her shaking hands. She hurried to the first available seat beyond the handicapped section and sank gratefully into a seat by the window.

What an awful day this had turned out to be! She had tried to make the best of Tarah as a project partner. She had tried to be nice to her and Cooper. Look what happened! She had planned to take home loads of pictures and a notebook full of good information. All she had were a few pictures and hardly any notes. Worse yet, that stranger seemed to threaten her. And now, on Monday, she had the ugly job of asking Ms. Reed for another partner.

The next day, Darcy, Jamee and Mom went to Aunt Charlotte's for dinner. A neighbor, Ms. Harris, was sitting with Grandma. About four times a year they went to Aunt Charlotte's townhouse as a kind of duty to family, even though none of them really wanted to go. "She is my only sister," Mom would point out. Darcy hated going to the upscale townhouse to eat one of Aunt Charlotte's strange gourmet meals featuring things like eggplant, tofu, and unusual, smelly cheeses.

"Your hair looks terrible, Mattie," Charlotte scolded the moment they came through the doorway. "Don't you ever go to the beauty salon? Lord knows you make a decent salary in that hospital. You don't need to have your hair looking like a bird's nest."

"I've got no time for beauty salons," Mom grumbled.

"Well, make time. There is nothing more important for a woman than attending to her appearance." Charlotte's critical gaze fell on Jamee next. "And you! You look like a homeless child who fished her wardrobe out of a dumpster! Now look at your sister. Darcy has the good sense to look neat and attractive."

Darcy did not want to be the one earning Aunt Charlotte's approval. Still, she smiled weakly, trying to be polite.

"Everybody at school dresses like this," Jamee said in her own defense. She flopped down on the sofa and began playing with Aunt Charlotte's Pekinese dog.

"Children today have no style," Charlotte continued as she lit the candles on her table. "They haven't a clue about giving good impressions to people who can help them up the ladder of success. Would I be an executive secretary in a major bank if I didn't present myself properly?"

Darcy waited for Aunt Charlotte to ask how Grandma was. After all, she was Grandma's daughter too. She hardly ever came over. She never even wanted to say hello to Grandma over the phone. One time, when Darcy's mother begged her to come over, Aunt Charlotte got an almost terrified expression on her face and said, "Oh! Don't ever pressure me to come over there again! Mattie, I cannot bear people in Mom's condition— I just can't bear them!"

"So, how are things at the hospital?" Charlotte asked her sister. "Are they still dumping all their paperwork on you?"

"Everybody is working hard in the ER," Mom said. "We've had staff cuts and more on the way. The workload is getting worse every day."

Aunt Charlotte changed the subject. "I cannot understand why you continue to live in that awful neighborhood, Mattie. I mean, it can't be good for your daughters to live among all those low-class people."

"Oh no," Mom said, "the girls have nice friends. Brisana is one of Darcy's friends, and she's a lovely girl. And your friends are nice too, aren't they, Jamee?"

"Yeah, right," Jamee said, glaring at the eggplant dish on the table.

"You see?" Charlotte said sharply. "She dresses in a slovenly way, and she has no manners. She doesn't even have the courtesy to look at me when she speaks to me."

"Jamee," Mom scolded, "don't mumble into your food when you're talking to someone."

Jamee looked up, her eyes narrow with resentment. "I don't even want to be here, okay? You act like you're better than we are. And every time we come here, you make the nastiest food!"

Aunt Charlotte recoiled in horror. "I will have you understand that I make gourmet meals which are raved over by all my friends. How dare you—"

"Jamee," Mom warned, "you'd better watch your mouth!"

"I won't!" Jamee yelled, glaring at Aunt Charlotte. "You never, ever come to visit Grandma. You never even visited when she was in her own little house. Sometimes Grandma would cry about it. Now Grandma is dying and Mom takes care of her, but you won't even come over to help for one lousy day in a month! You're selfish! You just sit in this ugly, stupid townhouse and spend all your money on ugly, stupid paintings that make me want to puke!"

"Jamee!" Mom wailed, but it was too late. Aunt Charlotte got up and wiped her lips with the corner of her fancy napkin.

"Mattie, please take your hateful, spoiled daughter and leave at once. And never bring her back until she learns to behave like a lady!"

Amid the clatter of Mom and Jamee getting up to leave, Aunt Charlotte came to Darcy's side and said, "I wish you didn't have to go. You have that certain something that your sister will never have: class. I'm afraid she takes after your good-for-nothing father!"

Darcy did not say anything. She hurried after her mother. Jamee was already racing down the stairs toward the car. When they all reached the car, Mom began bitterly scolding Jamee. "How could you embarrass me like that? It's bad enough Charlotte has always looked down on me, with her perfect life—'You need to get to the salon.' 'You should never have married that man in the first place.' And now you're giving her good cause to say that I'm a bad parent!"

Jamee crawled into the back seat, folded her arms, and closed her eyes. Darcy sat beside her mother up front. "Mom, Aunt Charlotte has no right to put you down," Darcy said. "You're a great nurse—you practically run that ER! You save people's lives every night.

You're a hero and a great Mom and a great daughter to Grandma. Aunt Charlotte just fools with a computer in an old bank, and she doesn't lift a finger for anybody but herself. She's got no right putting you down!"

Mom took her eyes off the road for a minute to look at Darcy. "Oh baby, what would I do without you?" Tears began to roll softly down her cheeks. "But the truth is, I'm no hero. I'm just trying to keep ahead of a mountain of paperwork and doing about one-third of the patient care that I ought to be doing. I'd need the arms of an octopus to meet all their needs. And I did blow it marrying your father. Maybe I was a bad wife, or he wouldn't have left me like that."

"Mom!" Darcy cried. "It wasn't your fault. It was *his* fault! He was like what Pastor Bromley says about people who desert their families: They're weak and selfish!"

Jamee was roused to join in the condemnation of their father. "Yeah, he was a jerk!"

"Maybe that's true," Mom said softly.

"It is, Mom," Jamee insisted. "What kind of a man sneaks away like that? What kind of a dirty coward does that?

Just because he fell for that stupid Janelle woman was no reason to dump us!"

"Jamee, what are you talking about?" Mom asked, in a horrified voice, nearly swerving the car into oncoming traffic.

"Oh, Mom," Jamee went on, rolling her eyes, "Janelle's niece, Deedra, goes to my school, and she told me the whole story. Her Aunt Janelle was a waitress at that diner where Dad used to eat breakfast. She told me how Dad would flirt with this young, pretty waitress. The next thing she knew, the two of them ran off to New York together. Deedra's been teasing me about it ever since. The other kids used to ask what happened to my daddy, and I'd make up some lies. But the truth is Dad left us for that young waitress."

Mom was really crying now, and Darcy wanted to strangle Jamee for what she said. Darcy and Jamee had discussed the true story a couple of years ago, but they had promised to keep silent out of respect for Mom's feelings.

"Oh Mom, stop crying," Jamee said crossly. "Men are slime. Boys too. Old Aunt Charlotte is pretty smart not to have anything to do with them. She just makes piles of money and takes trips to Paris and Madrid and takes care of herself instead of wasting time on men."

"You don't believe that's a good way to live," Darcy said. "It's just an empty life, that's all."

"What good is a full life if it's full of nothing but hurt and misery?" Jamee asked.

Mom was quiet for a few blocks. Then she said, "Jamee, when we get home, you're going to sit right down and write a note of apology to your aunt."

"I won't," Jamee snapped.

"Well, then you can just forget about me signing the permission slip for your cheerleader camp, and no mall on Saturday either," Mom said.

Jamee sighed deeply. "Ohhh, I'll write the stupid apology, but I won't mean it. And before I mail it, I'll spit on it!"

"You'd better not," Mom warned.

Darcy thought about her trouble with Tarah and Cooper all day Sunday afternoon and evening. She did not want to go see Ms. Reed and ask for a new partner. She wanted to find some way to make peace, to get things to where they were before that silly water bug incident at the tidal pool. But she did not know how to do it or if Tarah would even want to work with her again.

"Brisana," Darcy asked on the way to school Monday morning, "what should I do?"

"Darcy, after what that freak did to you, he ought to be suspended from school! I mean, you are totally crazy to have anything more to do with him and his stupid girlfriend," Brisana said.

"Brisana, don't call them names. I mean—" Darcy said softly. It was the first time she had ever spoken up against Brisana's treatment of others.

"Give me a break, Darcy! Don't tell me you *like* them? I mean, it's just like my father says. 'If you lie down with dogs, you'll get up with fleas.' Those two are low class. I don't know what my parents would even do if I brought home trash like Tarah Carson."

"Don't call her trash," Darcy replied. "It's just that she wasn't brought up like us, with manners and all. She's not really bad or anything."

"She's a fat cow, Darce! And she's got a nasty hair weave!" Brisana snapped.

"What's the matter with you? Don't you remember when we were sophomores last year and we rated the kids we'd see on a scale of one to ten? Remember, the tens were the highest? Well, Tarah Carson was among the zeros. She couldn't even make it to number one. Now, that's low class."

"Oh Brisana . . . I mean, it's not right to rate kids by numbers. And we weren't really serious about that. We were just acting silly," Darcy said.

"Come on, Darcy, some people are just beneath us, and that's all there is to it. And they belong in a special school with the other rejects. If I were you, I'd report what Tarah and Cooper did to you, how you almost died of fright when that bug was in your sweater, how they laughed at you. Maybe you should change it a little— tell them it was a black widow spider and luckily it didn't bite you, but they wanted it to bite you and they hoped you'd die. Then they'd both get transferred to that reject school, and we'll be rid of them."

"But, Brisana, it was just a water bug," Darcy protested.

"So what? How will they know the difference? It's your word against theirs," Brisana argued.

Darcy saw it then, the silver Toyota that she had seen near the tidal pool. It was parked across the street from Bluford High. "Brisana, look over there! That car was at the tidal pool on Saturday. The guy seemed to be watching me then, and there he is again!"

Brisana turned her head. "The windows are so dirty I can't make out who's at the wheel."

"The car's starting up, Brisana—try to get a look at the driver when it goes by," Darcy said.

The silver Toyota moved past them at moderate speed. "Some fat old guy," Brisana said. "He was wearing a baseball cap."

"Yeah, he was the other day too. I wonder what he's lurking around for," Darcy said, worried.

"Maybe he's one of Tarah's or Cooper's crummy relatives," Brisana suggested darkly. "They have hordes of uncles and cousins hanging around their messy houses. I'm telling you, Darcy, you're making a big mistake getting mixed up with those low-life people. I wouldn't be surprised if that fat guy in the car is an uncle of Cooper's, and he wants to sell drugs at the school or something."

Darcy frowned. "Brisana, Cooper's a jerk, but he doesn't do drugs. Neither does Tarah."

"Maybe not now, but give them a couple of years," Brisana said. "I'm telling you, girl, they're headed for drugs and gangs. Darcy, wake up! We have to stick together. We're the tens!"

Brisana went to her first class, and Darcy headed for biology. Hakeem Randall was entering class at the same time Darcy was. He seemed to smile right at her—his warm, dark eyes looked so friendly. But Darcy was not sure. Maybe she only imagined it. She would feel like such a fool to smile back when he was not even smiling at her, so she hurried past him to her desk.

As she sat down, Darcy noticed a small note taped to her desk. She always sat in the same place by the window, so whoever wanted to leave her a note would know where to put it. Darcy's hands shook a little as she opened the note. Maybe it was an apology from Tarah and Cooper. That would be so great. That would make everything okay again.

The note was not handwritten. Instead, somebody had cut out letters from a newspaper or magazine and pasted them together to form words:

You'll pay for what you did, Darcy.
You can run, but you can't hide.

Darcy stared at the note in stunned silence. It was obviously written by someone who hated her. Could Tarah and Cooper be this angry at her? Was it possible that Brisana was right after all, that these were dangerous people?

Or was this note placed on Darcy's desk by some kid acting for someone else—like the fat man in the silver Toyota? Was some deranged stranger after her?

Chapter 5

Tarah came into biology and sat in her usual place. Darcy swallowed hard and walked over to her desk. Before Darcy could say a word, Tarah sheepishly mumbled, "Hey, sorry about Saturday. It was a dumb thing Cooper did. Me too. Hope you're not still mad."

"Oh, it's okay," Darcy said, flooded with relief. She had dreaded this moment for so long, and now the problem was resolved. "I got some books from the library for our report. I came up with a good problem for our project—we can focus on what happens to the plant and animal life when the water level rises twelve inches."

"Works for me," Tarah said with a wide grin.

"We can observe things like mussels and scallops in the real shallow water, and clams and anemones in the deeper water," Darcy said.

"Huh? What was that last thing you mentioned?" Tarah asked.

"An anemone. They're like flowers under the water, red and pink and green. I saw a brooding anemone down at the tidal pool."

"What was it brooding about?" Tarah asked with a twinkle in her eye. "Somebody coming after it?"

Darcy had to laugh. "They can take care of themselves. They've got this mouth with ninety stinging tentacles."

"I thought you said they were pretty flowers! Ewwwww!"

Darcy had almost forgotten about the threatening note on her desk. In her relief at making up with Tarah, she found it hard to believe that either Tarah or Cooper had anything to do with the note. Even if they had, now that she and Tarah were reconciled, the trouble would be over. She decided to put it out of her mind along with the memory of the water bug down her back.

"Let bygones be bygones," Grandma always used to say. *"Carrying grudges is like carrying an open flame in your pocket. It's gonna burn you before it burns anybody else."*

When Darcy got home from school, her mother was taking a pie from the oven to cool. "Mom," Darcy asked in a worried voice, "won't you be late for work?" Usually the minute Darcy got home, Mom was racing out the door, car keys in hand.

"I'm going right now, baby. I just baked an apple pie for you girls for dessert tonight. Maybe Grandma will feel well enough for a little piece too. She used to love apple pie. She made the best apple pie in Pinellas County," Mom said. "Honey, my friend Rhonda is picking up the first few minutes of my shift tonight, so I've got some extra time. Tell me about school. How's it going?"

"Oh, everything is fine, Mom. I'm working on a science project on tidal pools, and it'll be a lot of fun. We're going to learn about all kinds of weird sea creatures."

"Sweetie, I'm sorry I didn't tell you girls the whole truth about your father. I was just so ashamed, you know," Mom said softly.

"It's okay, Mom. It doesn't change anything. He left. That's all that's important," Darcy said.

"It just shamed me so much that he ran off with another woman," Mom said.

"She was a real pretty little thing. Skinny, nice legs. And she was young! That girl was twenty-four, and I was almost forty and I looked it. I was carrying ten, fifteen pounds that had no business being on this body, and—"

"Mom, stop it!" Darcy snapped. "You were pretty and you still are, right to this day. It didn't have a thing to do with you. He was just no good."

"Oh, honey, don't say that. It's just that he was growing older too. That bothered him a lot—mid-life crisis, you know. He'd tell me all the time, 'Mattie, I'm in my forties. You know how old that is? No man in my family ever lived to be fifty, so I'm almost dead, and all I've ever done is sell vacuum cleaners and live in a crappy neighborhood.' He just sort of went crazy thinking he hardly had any time left, and he wanted something to make him feel young again. And she was it. I guess he must've thought if he had a twenty-four-year-old girl on his arm, then he must be a young man again somehow."

Glancing at the clock, Darcy hugged her mother tightly and kissed her cheek. "You'd better run now, Mom. Don't think about it anymore. It's over. And stop worrying about me and Jamee. We can handle it. Besides, how bad can life be when we've got your apple pie to eat?" Her mother gave her a weak smile. "I'll try to get Grandma to eat some too," Darcy continued. "Don't work too hard tonight, okay?"

"Depends on how many ambulances come screaming up to the ER, baby," Mom said, finally going out the door. As soon as she was gone, the telephone rang.

Jamee was not home yet. Sometimes she was late doing cheerleader practice, but she was pretty good about calling home when she was going to be very late.

"Hello?" Darcy said. There was no answer, but on the other end of the line there was a long, horrifying scream, the kind you hear in horror movies. Then the caller hung up. For an instant, Darcy was shaken, but then she thought it had to be a prank. Some fool had just played a Halloween sound-effects tape into the phone. Darcy did not think she knew anyone stupid enough to pull a stunt like that. Had she been randomly called by a stranger? Or was someone she knew trying to scare her? The same person who wrote that awful note?

Darcy forced the call out of her mind and went to Grandma's room. Grandma was very confused today. She thought she was a little girl again, living in her mother's house in Alabama. Darcy used to try to talk Grandma out of her confused notions, but now she just went along with whatever Grandma was thinking. It made her less agitated.

"Mama won't like it that I've stayed here past supper," Grandma said. "Mama wants us home by supper."

"It's all right," Darcy assured her.

"Mama says it's all right for us kids to have fun, long as we're home by suppertime," Grandma insisted.

"Yes," Darcy replied.

"Mama says the woods are full of bad things, like snakes. I saw one once," Grandma said, shuddering at the memory.

Darcy gave Grandma a small slice of apple pie. Grandma smiled and smacked her lips. "This is delicious. My Mama makes the best pies."

Darcy stayed with Grandma until she fell asleep. Then she headed into the kitchen to do some studying. A few minutes later, Jamee got home. She tried to race unseen to her room, but Darcy saw her. "Jamee!" Darcy cried, jumping up.

"What happened?" Jamee's left eye was almost swollen shut, and her cheek was scratched and bruised.

"We were practicing cheers and we were doing a pyramid, and I was at the top and fell, that's all," Jamee said. "It's no big deal. Why do you have to go and make a big deal out of everything?"

"Jamee, you're lying! I can always tell when you're lying. You got in a fight, didn't you?" Darcy demanded.

Jamee glared at Darcy. "Why don't you just leave me alone? Aren't things bad enough around here without you dogging me like a cop or something? Just leave me alone!"

"Jamee, if somebody hit you, I want to know about it," Darcy pleaded. "I don't want people beating up on my little sister!"

"What if somebody did punch me?" Jamee said. "So what? What are you gonna do about it? I fell down doing cheers, okay? That's what I'm saying went down, and you don't know any different, okay? So just mind your own business!" Jamee hurried into her room and slammed the door.

Darcy knew Jamee was not telling her everything. She decided to call

Alisha Wrobel, Jamee's old friend from school. Darcy rummaged through the phone book and found the number.

"Hi, Alisha, this is Darcy, Jamee Wills' sister. Listen, was there a fight at school today?"

"Um . . . a fight? I didn't see any fight. I was in the library during the free period and . . . I just don't know about any fight," Alisha said.

"Jamee said she fell down during cheerleading practice, but she's so banged up she looks as if somebody hit her," Darcy said. "Alisha, you're on the cheerleading squad too. Were you guys practicing today?"

"Today? Sorry. Gotta go. Mom's calling. Bye." The phone clicked in Darcy's ear.

Darcy went to Jamee's room and rapped on the door.

"Go away," Jamee yelled.

"Jamee, you gotta talk to me or I'm calling Mom," Darcy said.

After a few seconds, Jamee opened the door. "What do you want? Haven't you done enough? You messed it up for me with Bobby, and now you just wanna rub it in my face. Just leave me alone!"

"Did Bobby Wallace hit you?" Darcy demanded.

65

A frightened look came onto Jamee's wounded face. Her eyes grew enormous. "No, he didn't! Whoever told you that is a dirty liar. I was in his car for two minutes, and all he did was yell and cuss me out. If that little witch Alisha Wrobel said Bobby hit me, she's lying—she couldn't even see what happened in the car."

"Jamee, you're lying. You broke up with that punk, and he hit you!" Darcy stormed.

Panic showed in Jamee's eyes. "Don't stick your nose in this, Darcy. I'm warning you. You'll only make things worse. Somebody could get hurt!" Jamee turned and slammed the door in Darcy's face.

Darcy felt sick. As long as Jamee denied that Bobby had hit her, there was nothing Darcy could do. But it made Darcy furious to think that Bobby had worked out his rage on her little sister.

Darcy checked on Grandma and then went to clean up the kitchen. She washed the dishes, put them away, and leaned forward to close the kitchen curtains.

Then she saw the silver Toyota again. It was parked across the street from her building. The stocky man in the baseball cap sat at the wheel. "Oh my God," Darcy whispered. Thoughts flooded her mind. He knew where Darcy lived! He was here! Sometime during the night he could find a way to get inside the apartment! It would not matter how securely the doors and windows were locked. He could get in and be standing there in the darkness.

Darcy rushed to the telephone and called the police. She told them that for the last few days she had been followed by a man in a silver Toyota. Now he was parked across the street. The police sergeant told Darcy to lock the door and a squad car would be there in a few minutes.

Darcy watched from the window as a police car pulled in behind the silver Toyota. The Toyota started up when its driver saw the police car, but when he heard a loudspeaker advising him to stop, he did. Darcy watched as police approached on both sides of the car. It was dark outside, and Darcy's view was partially blocked by several parked cars. She struggled to see what was happening.

The man in the baseball cap handed some kind of I.D. out the window. The officers took their time checking it. Then the man must have been asked to step away from the car. As she watched, Darcy was trembling. She could not see the man clearly even when he was in the street because the officers surrounded him. They checked him for weapons, and it looked as if he did not have any. Then he got back in his car and waited while one of the officers came toward Darcy's apartment.

"Police," he said crisply at the door. Darcy opened it. "Are you Darcy Wills, the person who made the call on the silver Toyota?"

"Yes. Who is that man? What does he want? He's been at my school and everywhere I've been. Why is he stalking me?" Darcy asked with increasing agitation.

"He claims to be your father, miss," the officer replied calmly.

Darcy's heart pounded wildly. She gasped as if she were choking. "My father? No, it can't be! My father has been in New York for years!"

"He said his name is Carl Wills, and his I.D. checks out. He has no outstanding warrants. He said he has two daughters, a fourteen-year-old and a sixteen-year-old, that he hasn't seen in five years. I asked him to tell me what your birth date is. He said you were born on April sixth. Is that correct?"

"Yes, but . . . anybody could know that," Darcy stammered.

"Miss, I'm going to ask my partner to have the man step from the car and walk under the street lamp. You should be able to see him pretty well from here, enough to know if it could be your father," the officer said.

"But I haven't seen him in five years," Darcy said.

"Just take a good look," the officer said. "Is your mother home?"

"No. She's at work. There's nobody here but my sister and my Grandma, and Grandma's sick," Darcy answered.

"All right," the officer said. "Just take it easy."

Darcy watched the heavy man get out of the car again. He shuffled to the corner under a bright street light. Darcy remembered her father sprinting across a field after a baseball, as fast as a teenager. It couldn't be him, she told herself. Her father took such pride in his body, in keeping fit. He used to work out at the gym and brag about wearing the same clothes size he did as a teenager.

"My Daddy got fat and then he got old," Darcy remembered her father saying with a sharp laugh. *"I'm not going that route. No way."*

Now the man was standing directly under the light. For a moment he reminded Darcy of a pathetic, baggy-pants, two-bit clown caught in the footlights of a cheap theater. The man removed his baseball cap, revealing short gray hair, like the stiff bristle of stubby dead grass at the end of the summer.

Darcy's father had black hair, as black as the shiny surface of the black Mercedes he dreamed of and never got. Dad's skin was smooth as a just-ripe plum. This man had a pouchy face, like a balloon with most of the air leaked out. He had dark circles under his eyes. His whole body sagged like a partially-full garbage bag with the load shifting towards the bottom.

But the more she looked, the more Darcy saw something familiar in the man's face. "It's him. It's my father," she whispered.

"Well, what would you like for us to do, miss?" the officer asked, after radioing his partner that the man could return to his car.

"Tell him to go away, please," Darcy said. "Just tell him to go away." Tears blinded Darcy, and her shoulders shook.

"He said he was trying to work up enough courage to contact you. You don't want to talk to him—is that right?" the officer asked.

"Just tell him to leave us alone," Darcy sobbed.

"All right then. We'll advise him that he runs the risk of being arrested for stalking if he bothers you anymore. Would you like a restraining order?"

"What's that?"

"That's an order that officially warns a person to stay away from someone who's afraid of that person. If he violates the order, he could be immediately arrested. Your mother could talk that over with you tomorrow."

"No," Darcy responded. "But tell him to go away."

Just then, Jamee came out of her bedroom. The loud music in her room had prevented her from hearing Darcy's call to the police department. She looked shocked to find the police in the living room.

The officer looked at Jamee, then at Darcy. "What is that all about?" he asked, his gaze on Jamee's bruised face.

"I fell during cheerleader practice," Jamee said shrilly. "If she's told you something else, it's a lie!"

"Jamee," Darcy said, grabbing her sister's hand and pulling her to the window. "Look out the window at the Toyota—that's Dad. He was sitting out there and I didn't know who he was and I called the police. He's been trying to talk to us."

Jamee stared through the window. "That lump in the car? That fat guy? That's not my father. That's not Daddy. . . ." Jamee caught her breath, and her gasp ended in a sob. "Is it?"

Chapter 6

"Yeah, Jamee, it is," Darcy said.

"Ohhh," Jamee groaned, her hands clasped to her cheeks.

"Well, I'll go down there and tell him you don't want to be bothered," the officer said.

Darcy and Jamee watched as the officer returned to the Toyota and talked to their father for a few minutes. Darcy saw the officer take a slip of paper from her father's hand.

"He's coming back up here," Jamee said nervously. "The cop is coming back."

At the apartment door the officer gave Darcy the paper. It had a phone number written on it. Darcy always thought her father had beautiful handwriting. He had gone to a small grammar school down South where they were strict about penmanship. The phone number was written in his familiar fancy script. It brought a fresh rush of pain into Darcy's heart.

"He said he won't bother you anymore," the officer told them, "but if you ever want to contact him, this is the number to use, miss. He said he'd stay away from here and from your school. I don't think you need to worry about him annoying you again."

Darcy nodded and mumbled a "thank you" clutching the note in her fingers. The girls watched as the Toyota left, and then the police car. They could not tell if their father glanced up one more time at the apartment window.

Jamee walked over to the kitchen table and sat down. She looked stunned. "Why would he come back here after all this time?".

"I don't know," Darcy said. Memories flooded back like scenes from an old movie. Darcy remembered the days before her mother was forced to work long hours to keep a roof over their heads, before they moved into the smaller apartment to save money, before Grandma's crippling stroke. She recalled the barbecues in the backyard when the family lived in National City, and the trips to Tijuana when Daddy would buy the girls giant paper flowers, and they would eat rolled tacos from street vendors. Most of all, she remembered the hiking trips into the mountains. They would find tadpoles in the spring streams, and Daddy would explain how they turned into frogs. And he would put the girls on his shoulders and march along with everybody chanting "ribbit-ribbit-ribbit." And then there were the visits to the giant cedar tree where he dubbed Jamee a princess. And, just so Darcy would not feel neglected, Daddy would put his hand on her shoulder and declare, "You're a princess, too."

Unable to shake the images from her mind, Darcy looked at Jamee and asked, "Do you remember the hiking trips we used to take?"

"Yeah," Jamee said. "I think being there in the mountains was the last time I was really happy." She shook herself, as if to chase away the memories. "Why'd he have to come back like that— like a stranger in the night?"

Darcy shrugged. The heavy man in the Toyota seemed to have nothing to do with those good memories. He seemed no part of them. In a way, he just made things worse.

"What's Mom gonna say?" Jamee asked.

"I don't know," Darcy replied, "but we'll have to tell her."

"Maybe she'll want him back," Jamee said. "She never dated anybody. Plenty guys have liked her. You remember Chuck, the nurse from Jamaica? He really liked Mom. He sent her flowers and everything. But she never did go out with him. Maybe she still loves Dad."

"I don't think so," Darcy said.

"I don't ever want to see him in my entire life," Jamee asserted with sudden, unexpected passion. "I hate him. I wish he was dead. I wish we had gotten his death notice."

Darcy made hot cocoa and waited with Jamee for Mom to come home. Going to bed and trying to sleep after what had happened was out of the question.

"We're telling her tonight, huh?" Jamee asked.

"Yeah. I can't sleep on it tonight," Darcy said.

"Mom's gonna be shocked," Jamee added.

Right after midnight, Mom came home. She spotted Jamee's face as soon as she walked in the door. "Baby! What happened to you?" she cried, throwing down her purse and rushing to Jamee.

"Nothing, Mom. I fell at cheerleader practice," Jamee lied, "but something else has happened."

"Mama?!" Mom gasped, thinking something had happened to Grandma.

"No, no," Darcy said quickly, "Grandma is okay. She's sleeping. It's that Dad is back in town."

Mom grabbed a chair and sat down quickly. "Your father came here?"

"He was sitting in a car across the street. I got scared. He's been following me for days. I didn't recognize him, so I called the police, and they told me it was him," Darcy explained.

"Merciful Lord, after all these years," Mom cried, clasping her arms tightly and rocking back and forth as if in grief.

"I told the police to tell him to go away and leave us alone," Darcy said. "But he left this. It's his phone number." Darcy showed her mother the scrap of paper, then put it on the kitchen counter.

"You want to see him, Mom?" Jamee asked.

"Oh, my head is spinning from all this, honey. I'm so tired. I just want to shower and go to bed. I need to let this sink in. I just can't believe it. Tomorrow is a school day, so you girls got to go to bed too."

Looking dazed, Mom got up and walked toward the bathroom. Later on, when Mom was in her bedroom, Darcy heard her weeping. She knew Mom was trying to muffle the sounds by burying her face in the pillow. But just as they did years earlier when Dad abandoned the family, the racking sobs bubbled through the darkness.

At breakfast the next morning, Mom kept repeating to the girls that she could not believe their father came back without even calling or sending a letter.

"He's a low-life," said Jamee.

"Mom, he doesn't even look like himself anymore," Darcy said. "He's so overweight and so . . . old, like he hasn't taken care of himself in a long time."

Mom drank her coffee, her eyes welling with sorrow.

Darcy kept thinking about the past as she walked to school. When she had been very small, her father had made shadow puppets on the wall with his hands. He would make a snapping alligator with one hand and a hopping pig with the other. Every night the two creatures would race across the wall of the girls' bedroom while their father recited a silly rhyme.

> *"Hot diggety dog, gonna eat that hog,"*
> *Says the old gator who looked like a log.*
> *"Hot diggety dee, he can't catch me,"*
> *Says the roly-poly little piggy, who hopped up the tree.*

Darcy and Jamee would chuckle with glee as the shadow pig always leaped away from the snapping jaws of the alligator.

Lost in memories, Darcy did not see Cooper and his friends in front of the school. Noisy as usual, they were sitting on top of Cooper's pickup truck and peering from the shell. There was also a lot of other noise around the front of the school, including loud rap music from a red Nissan parked at the curb. As Darcy got closer to the Nissan, she could feel the rap's deep bass pulsing in the air, shaking the windows of nearby cars.

Think hard, think fast,
Today might be your last,

chanted the rapper as Darcy passed the red car.

Man you better try,
Maybe you gotta lie,
Maybe you gonna die,
Ain't it a shame?
You got no one to blame,
When you're six foot under ground,
And lookin' up instead of down.

Just as Darcy got ready to cross the street, she heard the sound of an engine revving up loudly behind her. She turned and instantly the red Nissan sprang to life and blocked her path. Bobby Wallace leaned out the window. "Wanna talk to you, girl," he barked.

"I'm late for school," Darcy snapped. "Get out of my way."

"Better watch your mouth," Bobby snarled. "You in a lotta trouble for messin' me and Jamee up. We had a good thing, and you went spreadin' lies. I want you to fix it, you hear what I'm sayin'?"

"Are you crazy?" Darcy cried. "You think I want my sister hanging around with you? She was stealing for you, and when she broke up with you, you smacked her around. I wish you were in jail. If you touch her again, I'll make sure that's where you end up!"

Bobby's friend, who had been driving the Nissan, jumped from the car and came around, moving menacingly toward Darcy.

"You think little old Jamee's face looked bad?" Bobby sneered. "You won't wanna look in the mirror tomorrow when I get through with you."

Darcy tried to run around the Nissan, but Bobby, out of the car now, grabbed her wrist. His friend took out a knife and flashed it at her. "You and me gonna get in the car and go for a drive and talk," Bobby said, turning up the car's stereo to drown out the sound of Darcy's screams.

"Maybe you gonna die!" the rapper repeated.

Darcy yanked on her wrist, trying to pull free. Up ahead she saw students streaming into Bluford High, laughing and chattering. Nobody seemed to see the drama blocked by the red Nissan.

"Get your hands off me!" Darcy screamed as loud as she could, swinging her free arm and kicking at Bobby's shins. "Let me go!"

Darcy saw Bobby's hand coming at her face like a heavy club. It was all a blur after that. Cooper must have heard her scream even over the rap music because he and three of his buddies were all over Bobby and his friend. The hand aimed at Darcy's face never connected. Cooper and his crew pounced on Bobby and his friend, throwing them to the ground, as the rap music howled.

Ain't it a shame?
You got no one to blame,
When you're six foot under
    ground,
And lookin' up instead of
    down.

Beaten and bloody, Bobby and his friend crawled into the Nissan and took off. By that time Tarah and some other kids were there, cheering. "Way to go, Coop!" Tarah yelled above them all, helping Darcy up. "Little punks got what they deserved!"

"Thanks," Darcy said to Cooper and the other boys.

"It's fun knocking bullies upside their heads," Cooper laughed.

"I was so surprised Cooper would help me like that," Darcy admitted to Tarah later on.

"Shows how much you know, girl," Tarah scoffed. "Coop might get lousy grades, and he might act a little silly sometimes, but he's got heart. He won't let no sister get messed up by some thugs. Coop is one of the good guys. He wants to be a fireman when he finishes school. They're always saving folks. That's Coop."

A number of kids had seen what happened in front of the school, and by afternoon Bobby and his friend were disciplined. The principal, Ms. Spencer, told Darcy that Bobby had been suspended for three days. She also explained that Bobby admitted to leaving the note on Darcy's desk and making the prank phone call to her house. If he caused any more trouble, Ms. Spenser said, he would be expelled.

Darcy breathed a sigh of relief when she learned what had happened to Bobby. Walking home later that day, she thought about her run-in with Bobby and his friend. She could not remember ever being so afraid in her life. She had to catch her breath every time she thought about how that encounter with him could have turned out if not for Cooper.

Near home, Darcy looked for the silver Toyota. She half expected to see it. She did not know exactly how she felt when it wasn't there.

Chapter 7

At school the next day, Darcy thanked Cooper again for rescuing her from Bobby and his buddy. Cooper turned her gratitude aside with a joke. "Wasn't me done it, girl. It was that kick of yours. Man, you chased them away all by yourself!"

"Oh Coop," Tarah scolded, "stop dissin' your own self. You're a hero and you know it."

"A hero?" Cooper repeated, his eyes huge.

"Sure. Like John Wayne," Tarah said. "My Daddy loves those old John Wayne movies on TV. That's who you're like, Coop. John Wayne, only darker."

Cooper began to swagger around and imitate John Wayne's famous walk. "Gather 'round, pilgrims," Cooper said in his best John Wayne voice. "Here I am, a big black John Wayne come to town to right all the wrongs you dudes been pilin' up. Only I ain't got a horse. Anybody want to loan me a horse?"

Just then, Brisana came walking along. She glanced briefly at Cooper and Tarah and ignored them. Looking directly at Darcy, she asked, "Want to eat lunch with me at the usual place?"

"It's a nice place for lunch," Darcy said to Tarah and Cooper. "You guys want to join us?"

Brisana began gesturing wildly behind Cooper's and Tarah's backs, trying to make Darcy understand that she was not in the least interested in all four of them eating lunch together. Tarah and Cooper could not help noticing Brisana's message. "Go on, Darcy," Tarah said, "go and have lunch. See you later. We like it right here." Tarah looked hurt, but Darcy admired how cool she was about it.

"Oh, go ahead, Bris," Darcy answered. "I think I'll stay here today and eat with these guys."

Tarah looked at Darcy and declared, "You don't have to do that."

"I want to," Darcy said. "Catch up with you later, Brisana."

Brisana hurried off as if she could not move fast enough.

As soon as Brisana left, Cooper said, "Oh, I get it. You feel sorry for us. I mean, it's like when the social worker comes to check on the neighbor lady who's on disability. She acts like she just loves to sit down and talk, but deep down she's lookin' down on that lady." Scowling, Cooper added, "Listen, sistah, you don't have to be tight with us."

"What if I want to?" Darcy said, surprised by her own cool. "What if I really want to?"

"Well, then," Tarah said, "that's different." A big grin spread over her face.

As Darcy ate lunch with Tarah and Cooper, other regulars joined them, kids Darcy had little to do with in the past. They had often passed Darcy in the halls, at the library, even sat beside her in some classes, but they remained strangers. There was Keisha, whose parents owned and operated a tiny neighborhood grocery store. And there was Hakeem Randall, with a guitar slung over his shoulder. Once, when he sat off by himself, strumming and singing, Darcy had almost walked over to tell him how good he sounded. But she didn't.

Now he sat beside her, talking with Cooper about football. And there was also Shariff, a Sudanese boy who had just arrived at school, and Sonia, who quietly told Darcy that she had never liked Bobby Wallace.

When Hakeem finished his sandwich, he picked up his guitar and started playing. It seemed when he sang and played, his shyness disappeared, but he never met Darcy's admiring gaze. He sang lyrics he made up himself.

*You're starting to sound like bad
    dreams,*
The ones that've tangled my mind,
*I'm starting to be fearful of
    darkness,*
*Seems like you come back all the
    time.*

Darcy thought Hakeem was too fine for words. When he finished his song, at last he looked right at her, but then Darcy looked away. She was as shy as he was!

Yet, listening to Hakeem's song, Darcy almost felt she could tell him anything, even things about her family. In all the time she was at Bluford High, Darcy had never talked to anyone, not even Brisana, about her father and the hurt he had caused. Brisana's father was a bank official. Once, he was out of work for several months, and Brisana was so embarrassed she did not tell Darcy. Darcy found out from someone else. Brisana's mother was a clothes buyer for a pricey department store. Soon Brisana's family would have enough money to leave this neighborhood. Brisana could go to a better school, one where just about everybody was a "ten."

Darcy had been ashamed to talk about her vanished father. Nothing truly awful ever happened in Brisana's life. It happened only among the "low-life" people. In their world, fathers ran away, people drank too much, there was poverty. Darcy had hidden her pain from Brisana so Brisana would not think she was a "low-life" too. But Darcy ached to talk, really talk with a friend about how bad she felt.

After school, Darcy found Tarah shooting baskets in the court behind the gym. Mom did not have to go to work as early today, so Darcy did not need to rush home. "Hi, Tarah. You like basketball?" Darcy asked, sitting down on a bench.

"Yeah. Who knows, maybe it'll be my ticket to college one of these days. Sure beats flippin' burgers." Darcy looked at her with surprise. "I know what you're thinkin'," Tarah said as she expertly dribbled the ball. "I'm too fat. But the way I see it, that can change. Coach Williams says I have potential," she stated with obvious pride.

"Girl, you go for it," Darcy said. "My Grandma always says, 'Jump at the sun, and you might just catch a star.'" The two girls smiled at each other and sat on a nearby bench. It was October, but it was hot that afternoon. Soon the temperatures would cool, perhaps suddenly. But right now it was even warm in the shade.

"You know what, Tarah?" Darcy said, the words rushing out like water suddenly released from a dam, "My Dad just came back into our lives after being gone for five years. It's just so weird. I don't even know what I feel."

"That's wild," Tarah said with concern. "You mean he just popped in?"

"Out of nowhere. He started lurking around, and I didn't even know it was him. I called the police, and they told me it was him. He left Mom five years ago for somebody else, and it tore us all up. Especially my sister. She was only nine, and she worshiped Dad. She's sorta been lost ever since, and now he's back—almost like a ghost of somebody you thought was dead," Darcy said.

"So what's your Mom say? She gonna let him come back or what?" Tarah asked.

"I don't know what she's feeling. I told the police to tell him to stay away from us, and Mom seemed okay with that. He left a phone number in case we wanted to call him, but what would we say? I sure don't know what I'd say." Darcy shook her head. "I mean, when he first left I cried about it, and then I was mad and I hated him, and then I didn't feel anything. Maybe just an empty feeling, like there was some big hole inside me somewhere and it wouldn't close up." Darcy could not believe how much of herself she was revealing to a girl she hardly knew. It was one thing gossiping about another girl's father being a drunk, or somebody's sister getting pregnant. But now Darcy was admitting that there was a large, dark secret in her own family, that Dad had ripped a hole so big and deep that maybe her own little sister was being pulled into its terrible darkness.

"So what are you gonna do?" Tarah asked.

"Nothing, I guess. I just wish it could all be the way it was before. My sister, Jamee, says she wishes Dad was dead. I guess that would make it easier. I mean, I might be able to forgive him if he was dead," Darcy said, twisting the hem of her shirt.

"You wanna talk to him?" Tarah asked.

"I'd like to ask him why he did such a thing to us. I'd like to hear it from his own mouth. I guess I know what happened, but I'd like to hear him try to explain. Maybe I want to see him squirm and be ashamed and feel as rotten as I do, but still, it'd be so horrible to actually hear it—to know this guy I hate is someone I used to love so much."

"You oughta see him," Tarah said firmly. "Get it all out. Sometimes good people do rotten things. Then they realize the mistakes they made and turn their lives around. Sometimes bad people do good things too. We had a neighbor who was real bad—a drug dealer. He gave a kidney to a little boy who was dyin'. And then the guy got a sickness that messed up his other kidney and he didn't mind

92

'cause he said he can die feelin' proud. He said he lived his whole life for his own rotten self, but he got the chance to die for somebody else and he was glad. You can't give up on people, girl, you hear what I'm sayin'? God don't give up on us, no matter what we do. So where we get off givin' up on each other?"

"But Tarah, nothing he says will make it better. Don't you see that? What could he say to make it okay that he left us like that? The thought that he thinks he can crawl back into our lives and be a father and a husband again just makes me sick," Darcy said.

"Maybe he just passing through, girl. Wants to make amends and then go back to wherever he came from. Maybe even he's sick or dying or something, and he wants to tie up loose ends. Lots of folks try to fix stuff when they're dyin'," Tarah said.

Darcy leaned against the brick wall of the gym and closed her eyes. She felt as if confusion and grief were overtaking her. A dry, rasping sob flew from her throat. Suddenly she felt Tarah's arms around her, warm and comforting. Into Tarah's shoulder, Darcy cried big, violent sobs, like nothing that had escaped her for years.

"We all got hurts," Tarah said. "If we ain't got them now, they'll be comin'."

Tarah's hug was more comforting than Darcy ever imagined. It was as if she had left a small part of her sorrow with someone else, and now what was remaining would be easier to carry.

When Darcy got home from school, she found Jamee more withdrawn than ever. Darcy took a deep breath before speaking. She knew that now, more than ever, she had to choose her words carefully. She did not want to upset her sister again.

"Jamee, I know that you really cared about Bobby Wallace," Darcy began. "I remember how you told me that he gave you his picture and said you were his special girl. And I know that all the girls at school were probably jealous of you because you had a boyfriend from Bluford High who drove a cool car. But Bobby wasn't the right guy for you. Any guy who puts his hands on you is bad news."

Jamee did not say a word. She just sat there flipping through a magazine. It hurt Darcy to even look at her blackened eye and swollen cheek. But as bad as the bruises were on the outside, Darcy knew it was the inside that was really hurting in Jamee. Mom did not seem to notice that anything was wrong, though. She was so preoccupied with the news of Dad's return that she barely saw what was happening to Jamee.

"I've made up my mind," Mom said at dinner. "I went through a few hours when I had a strong desire to call your father. I'm past that now. What good would it do? He'd offer lame excuses for what he did, like he always did. He'd bring up all the old stuff again, how it shamed him that I made more money than him, and how that made him feel less than a man. How I didn't support him in those get-rich-quick schemes, and how I wasn't the loving wife he'd hoped for. I don't need to be brought down by all that."

"I understand, Mom," Darcy said.

"Yeah," Jamee agreed, "who wants that bum back in our lives anyway?" Jamee's lower lip trembled as she spoke. Darcy saw something in Jamee's eyes— the sudden dulling of a spark of hope. A hope, however far-fetched and wild, had risen in her heart when her father came back. This much had been obvious to Darcy.

The daddy who had once treasured Jamee had reappeared. Maybe, by some unknown magic, he could make her feel special again. Jamee would never admit to such a thing in words, but Darcy knew her well enough to see hope flicker in her brown eyes. In Jamee's world of ear-shattering hip-hop music, of a much loved, now almost lost Grandma, a boyfriend who hurt and betrayed her, a father who abandoned her, even a slim thread of hope flared bright against the darkness. But now it too had gone out.

Jamee usually ate her dessert right after dinner, especially when it was Mom's apple pie, but she left the table tonight without touching it. "I've got to study for a history quiz," she said. Mom seemed very pleased. Mom winked at Darcy as if to say, *"See, her interest in school is finally blooming. She's hitting her stride like I said she would."*

Darcy thought about it. She could not recall hearing Jamee say anything about taking history this marking period. She shrugged her shoulders, deciding to ask Jamee about that later.

After Mom left for work, the drumbeat of dismal music flowed from Jamee's room again. The lyrics of the rap were drowned out by the brain-busting beat of charging rhythms. It was just as well. The lyrics were about doom and gloom. It sounded as though the music was celebrating the end of the world.

Cooper agreed to drive everybody to the tidal pool on Saturday. This time Hakeem Randall joined them, which made Darcy both excited and nervous. She was glad that she had decided to put on a little lip gloss before she left the house. Tarah's mom packed two baskets full of fried chicken, rolls, and potato salad. The four ate heartily before trooping down to the water's edge.

Tarah and Cooper clambered onto the rocks for a better view, leaving Darcy and Hakeem by themselves.

"You play the guitar really well," Darcy said.

"Thanks," Hakeem said. "I . . . I've seen you around school. I wanted to talk to . . . to you a coupla times, but—"

"It's hard for me to meet new people," Darcy said, watching a purple sea urchin slip through the shallow water.

"Yeah, me too," Hakeem said. "I'm always saying the wrong thing, or, y'know, not knowing what to say."

"I guess we're sorta the same then," Darcy said, looking up at him and smiling shyly.

Hakeem smiled back. "I know this is pretty sudden, but I'd really like to hang out with you some more. How about we go see Alada together Friday after school?"

"What's Alada?" Darcy asked, her heart thumping happily.

"Oh, it's a really fly local band. They play reggae and hip-hop that keeps the audience jumpin'," he explained enthusiastically.

Darcy's heart was absolutely galloping now. Hakeem was so close in the cramped space on the sand that she could almost feel his warm breath on her cheeks. His eyes seemed to be filled with tiny golden lights, or was that just Darcy's imagination? She had been so sad, so miserable and bewildered over Jamee's problems, Grandma slipping away, Dad's strange reappearance—and now, all of a sudden, Darcy felt a completely unexpected surge of joy.

"So, you wanna go?" Hakeem persisted.

"Sure, sounds like fun. I'll ask my mom and let you know tonight."

"Cool," Hakeem agreed contentedly. He smiled again, a wondrous smile. Darcy had never seen one quite like it before. The lights in his eyes sparkled like gold dust.

Chapter 8

"Mom, I met a boy, " Darcy blurted out at the dinner table that night.

"Really, sweetheart?" Mom replied.

"Yeah, his name's Hakeem Randall. He goes to my school, and he's real cute. We got to talk this afternoon for the first time because he came with us to the tidal pool. And get this, he asked me to go to a concert with him after school Friday. Can I, Mom? I won't get home too late," she promised.

"Well, I suppose so. Are any of your friends going too?"

"I don't know for sure, Mom, but Hakeem said Alada's the hottest thing going this year, so I bet Tarah and Cooper are gonna be there."

"Just make sure you're home by 10:00," her mother said. "I'm working the late shift that night, so I'll be here when you get back. You can tell me all about what happens," she added with a smile.

"Thanks, Mom," Darcy grinned and floated off, wrapped in private daydreams.

Jamee, however, was not nearly so thrilled. She left the dinner table and went to Grandma's room. She hardly ever did that anymore. When Grandma was well and lived in her own little house, Darcy and Jamee spent a lot of time there. Jamee would race in first and fly into Grandma's arms. But now that Grandma was so confused and different, Jamee avoided her most of the time.

Darcy heard voices from Grandma's room.

"Grandma, do you remember hiking and the mountains?" Jamee asked in a forlorn voice.

"Is that you, Jamee?" Grandma asked.

"Yeah, it's me," Jamee said. "Do you remember, when we'd go hiking, and then sometimes go back at night just to look at the stars and the moon? Remember how bright the moon was, Grandma?"

"I'm glad we went hiking," Grandma said. "The air smells so nice. It's the pines, you know."

"Yeah," Jamee mumbled, sounding incredibly sad.

"I can't see the moon, Jamee. It's so dark. I can't see the moon at all. Tell me what it looks like."

"It's big, real big, and the Moon Monster is about ready to come down. He's lonely, Grandma. He's so lonely. He wants to catch somebody and take that person back to the moon so he has somebody to talk to."

"Did you girls and your Daddy catch plenty of fish? Carl is such a good fisherman. Mmm, don't they smell good, child?"

Grandma must have fallen asleep then, and Jamee left the room without saying anything. She went to her room and closed the door.

Friday began like an ordinary day. Jamee left for school with her backpack at the regular time. She did not eat much breakfast, but then she usually didn't. She did not talk much, but that was not unusual either. Darcy did not pay much attention to her because she was excited about going to the concert that evening with Hakeem.

Thinking about Hakeem crowded most everything out of Darcy's mind. She did not even think much about her father. Darcy had gone on a couple of dates before, but never with somebody she really liked, someone like Hakeem. After English, she saw him in the hallway, as always. But this time, she looked him in the eyes and smiled.

"Are we still on for the concert?" he asked.

"We certainly are," Darcy said. "I can't wait!"

"I . . . I've been saving my money to buy a motor bike, and I'm almost there," Hakeem said, "but not quite yet. And since we can't have Coop cartin' us all over town, we're gonna have to ride the bus to the concert. Hope you don't mind."

"That's fine," Darcy replied. The truth was, she did not care if they had to walk to the concert. She just wanted to be with Hakeem.

"Well, the concert starts at 7:00, so I could meet you at your house at 6:15, and we can walk to the bus stop together," Hakeem suggested.

"That'll be great." Darcy smiled, her heart leaping in her chest.

Darcy and Hakeem took the bus to the little club downtown where the band was performing. As they worked their way through the ecstatic crowd to get closer to the band, friends here and there shouted out greetings.

As much as Darcy enjoyed the music, she enjoyed being with Hakeem even more. His company put a glow on everything. After the concert, they strolled around downtown. Darcy thought the nice cafés and shops were a welcome change from her neighborhood. And being there with Hakeem only made the evening more magical.

Hakeem was still flying high off the music. "Man, weren't they incredible? That's what I want to do. Get up in front of a crowd, set the beat, get people jammin' and lost in the music," he said wistfully.

"I can picture you up on stage," Darcy said. "Your voice is great, and so is your guitar playing," she added, smiling.

Hakeem looked directly at Darcy. "You know, I never thought you would be so nice. I feel good with you, Darcy. I feel comfortable. I don't feel comfortable right away with many people. I mean, you seemed stuck up when I didn't know you. But I guess you're like me—just shy."

Hakeem and Darcy arrived at her apartment just before 10:00. They hesitated together at the door for a few minutes. Darcy was very nervous, but she had to show him how much she liked him, so she pulled Hakeem's face down and kissed his cheek. Then Darcy grinned and ran inside. She knew Mom would be anxious to leave for her night shift at the hospital.

"Did you have a nice time, baby?" Mom asked. She was already dressed, car keys in hand.

"Yeah, Mom. It was wonderful," Darcy said. She did not hear rap music from Jamee's room. "Is Jamee home?"

"No, she isn't," Mom said matter-of-factly. "She's spending the night with Alisha." Mom gave Darcy a quick peck on the cheek and hurried out. Darcy was surprised to hear that Jamee was spending the night over there. Jamee and Alisha had a falling out weeks ago when Jamee began hanging out with Bobby Wallace.

Darcy decided to call Alisha's house. Alisha's mother answered the phone. When Darcy asked for Jamee, Mrs. Wrobel said, "I haven't seen your sister in weeks. Alisha isn't even here tonight. She's over at her father's for the weekend."

Darcy rushed to Jamee's room. It was locked, but Darcy found a spare key and got in quickly. Darcy's hands shook as she turned the lock. The room looked the same, nothing unusual. But when Darcy checked the closet, she found all Jamee's favorite clothing gone—the T-shirts, the jeans—even her CDs. Jamee had left the nice dresses her mother had bought for her—the ones she never wore. She had left the family picture albums, the school books, the mosaic jewelry box Darcy had given her for her birthday, the beaded jewelry Jamee had spent hours making for herself.

Darcy called every number she had for Jamee's friends or acquaintances. She even called Bobby Wallace's house. His mother said he was with his grand-parents in Arizona. Nobody had seen or heard anything about Jamee's where-abouts. Darcy called the phone number her father had given them, but there was no answer.

Darcy did not want to bother her mother at work, but she had no choice. "Mom, Jamee is gone."

"Gone? Baby, I told you she was spending the night with—"

"Mom! No! That was a lie. I called Alisha's house, and she wasn't even supposed to be there. Jamee took all her favorite stuff and she ran away, Mom."

"Ran away? Lord in heaven, why would she do that? She's only a baby. She was fine at breakfast. Nothing was bothering her, nothing in the world." Mom was crying. Her voice was shaking. "I'll be home as soon as they can get someone to take my shift."

"Okay, Mom. I'll make some more calls," Darcy said.

Darcy finally talked to two of Jamee's classmates, who returned her calls. They both said Jamee had been in class as usual. Nobody had noticed anything strange about her. She always sat in the back, so nobody paid much attention to her. "Was she upset or anything?" Darcy asked. Neither of the classmates had noticed anything, but then they did not know Jamee that well.

Darcy figured that Jamee had packed everything last night in the suitcase

Mom had bought for her two years ago. It was for the trip they had taken to San Francisco to see cousins. Jamee probably packed and stashed the suitcase in her closet without anybody noticing. Mom was napping. Darcy was distracted. Who would have seen her?

When Darcy's mother came home, she called the police. An officer came to their apartment and took a missing-person report. Foul play was not suspected. It looked as if Jamee was just another runaway teenager. "Often a girl like that will hide out with friends for a few days, then surface," the officer said.

"We've called around everywhere," Darcy said.

"There's one other thing," Mom said. "A week ago, her father showed up after five years. He left this phone number. I'm sure Jamee wouldn't have gone to him, but I suppose you should check there too."

After the officer left, Mom began to cry. "How could she do something like this to us? How could that child hurt this family after it's already been hurt so much? I've done my best for her. I've struggled for my children, struggled alone. How could she do such a thing?"

Darcy hugged her mother and whispered, "She'll be back. She just wasn't thinking straight, Mom."

"She was a happy girl, wasn't she? She wasn't doing all that well in school, but I didn't nag her about it. I didn't make demands on you girls, did I? I just let you set your own pace. I never criticized her friends or made her stop playing that loud music that gave me a headache. I gave her freedom. What did I do wrong?"

"Nothing, Mom. She's probably already sorry and on her way home," Darcy said.

The next day, Saturday, Darcy tracked down Cindy, one of Jamee's friends who was part of the group of kids that hung out near the school. Cindy and her mother lived in an apartment about six blocks west of the school. Darcy could hear the muffled sound of a TV as she walked up to the worn door and knocked. Cindy was home alone, and she looked a little embarrassed to be caught in her hair rollers and bathrobe. Darcy asked her about Jamee.

"I'm not surprised that she ran. I wanna do it too," Cindy said. "Jamee is sick of a lotta things. She hated school, she's got problems at home. I guess all of it just got to her, so she took off to get away. Once Jamee talked about catching a bus and just going as far as it could take her. She's probably thinking there's got to be something better than what's around here. People getting shot or using drugs or parents leaving their kids. It can't all be like this." Darcy could see in her eyes that Cindy was speaking for herself as much as she was speaking for Jamee. Darcy thanked her and left.

In the afternoon, Darcy got together with Tarah, Cooper and Hakeem. She told them what Cindy said.

"Whoa," Cooper said, "little girl like Jamee could get in big trouble."

"Maybe she didn't get that far yet," Hakeem said. "Maybe she's still close by. Why don't we just drive around and take a look? We might see her in front of a hot dog stand or something."

"Yeah," Tarah chimed in. "Maybe she never left the 'hood. Or even if she did take a bus downtown, maybe she lost her nerve after that. She could be sittin' in the bus station right now."

"Come on," Cooper said. "We can ride in my truck." They all piled in and Cooper drove slowly around the neighborhood, stopping where groups of kids gathered. Then they headed for downtown. The area around the bus station was crowded. There they found the usual mix of people, men in shabby clothes, a few military people, and some teenagers. But Jamee was not one of them.

Cooper parked, and they went into the bus station and looked at the people who sat waiting on benches. They did not find Jamee. Darcy did not really expect it would be that easy.

Down the street from the bus station, there was a group of teenagers gathered in front of a video store.

Darcy reached into her wallet. She pulled out a small photograph of Jamee that Mom had taken last year and walked over to them. Hakeem, Cooper, and Tarah followed her.

"We're looking for my little sister. She disappeared yesterday, and no one knows where she is. Here's her picture. Anybody seen her?" Darcy asked. The kids leaned in close to get a good look at the tiny photograph.

One boy with a shaved head studied the picture carefully. "Try looking down at the canyon," he said. "Lotsa kids and runaways head down there at night."

"Thanks, man," Hakeem said, as the boy walked away.

"The canyon?" Tarah asked, unable to hide the alarm in her voice.

Darcy had heard of such a place before, but only in news reports and rumors about drugs and crime.

"That place is no joke," Cooper explained. "Let's hope she ain't there."

A cold breeze began to blow as they climbed back into Cooper's truck and headed toward the canyon on the outskirts of the city. The sun was getting lower, and a thick line of clouds was beginning to crawl into the sky from the west. Darcy felt a sudden chill. She tried to convince herself that Jamee was somewhere warm and safe. But as the truck got farther and farther from the neighborhood, Darcy shuddered at the thought that her sister might be alone in the cold and darkening hills.

Chapter 9

"Your sister's not gonna be in the canyon hangin' with those losers," Tarah scoffed. "They do drugs and fight and—"

"I just want to make sure," Darcy said, swallowing hard.

Cooper drove into the park, and the four of them walked down toward the canyon, toward the murmur of voices and the smell of marijuana.

"Look," Cooper said, "lemme do the talkin', okay?" He led the way.

Darcy could not make out the faces of anybody in the canyon. Many wore ponchos or were wrapped in blankets against the night's chill. Garbage-bag tarps sheltered a pair leaning against a pine tree. Cooper passed Jamee's picture around, and then he returned to the other three. "She's not here. Never was. They were straight-up with me."

113

"I'm so scared," Darcy said as they walked back to the truck. "What if we never find her? What if she just disappears like those kids you see pictures of on flyers, the ones who disappeared years ago? What if we never even find out if she's dead or alive?"

Hakeem put his arm around Darcy's shoulders and pulled her gently against himself. "Don't think that way. She's gonna be back. She's just hanging out somewhere."

"She took all her favorite clothes," Darcy cried.

"Kids do stupid things, you know," Hakeem reminded her.

"Yeah," Tarah agreed. "I ran away when I was 'bout thirteen. My Dad is really strict, and I wasn't havin' any more of it, you hear what I'm sayin'? I was outta there. I hid in my cousin's basement for three days. Then they found me and hauled me home and my Dad took off his belt and whupped me silly. He goes, 'This is 'cause I love you, Tarah Lucille,' and then he whupped me. I couldn't sit down for a week after that! But I sure was glad to be back home."

They drove around for another hour, looking at every forlorn and spaced-out kid they saw. But there was no sign of Jamee, and finally Cooper and the gang headed back to Darcy's apartment.

"It'll be okay, Darcy," Hakeem said as they pulled up in front of her apartment. He leaned over and brushed a kiss over Darcy's ear. "I'm praying for you and your sister. It'll be okay."

Darcy was getting out of the truck when she saw the silver Toyota across the street. Darcy's father got out when he saw her.

"Who's that?" Hakeem asked as the heavy man approached them.

"That's my Dad," Darcy said, feeling her palms beginning to sweat. She had not spoken to him since he had gone.

"But I thought he left your family years ago," Hakeem replied.

"He did," Darcy whispered.

Hakeem looked surprised, and Darcy wanted to explain everything to him, but not now. Hakeem seemed to take the hint, and she was grateful that he did not ask any more questions.

Darcy stared at her father in the brightness of Cooper's headlights. His face was puffy and swollen, and his eyes were red. Darcy could not help thinking he looked like the loser of a boxing match that had lasted for years.

"I know I shouldn't be here," Carl Wills said, "but the police called me about Jamee being missing."

Darcy was torn between the small signs of familiarity, the soft brown eyes like tawny velvet, that had been so comforting when he told her bedtime stories, and the bloated face that bore no resemblance to the person he once was.

Darcy had often wondered what she would say to her father if she ever met him again. She had wondered what wild, conflicting emotions would whirl through her heart. But now, in her sorrow and worry over Jamee, there was little emotion over meeting her father. Darcy simply stared at him the way tourists might stare at a monument they were curious about.

Finally, Darcy's father said in a deep, anguished voice, "It wasn't over me coming back, was it? That isn't what made her run, is it? May God strike me dead if I'm the cause of it."

Darcy could not speak. She was grateful to Hakeem for standing beside her. He waved to tell Cooper and Tarah to drive away.

"Call me as soon as you know anything," Tarah called.

"Good luck, Darcy!" Cooper added, before driving off.

Hakeem took Darcy's hand and said, "Darcy, if you don't want to talk to your father, I will. I'll find out if he knows anything about where your sister is."

Darcy hesitated for a moment, and Dad finally spoke up. "We could go somewhere and talk," he suggested. "Me, you, and your friend. There's a diner not far from here."

"What do you want to do?" Hakeem asked Darcy in a gentle voice.

Darcy nodded. "I'll go," she said. She and Hakeem squeezed into the front seat of her father's car. Judging by the clutter on the back seat, he had been living there. Shirts and pants were piled next to stuffed bags and boxes.

Darcy sat there, her mind caught up in memories of birthday parties, rides on roller coasters, trips to the zoo, Dad holding her over his head while she screamed with joy. Of the night when they knew he was gone, Mom sobbing, Jamee screaming. Of the hopes that he would return and the slow, painful way all hope died as time built impenetrable barriers.

Could Jamee have called him of all people and told him where she was going? Could she have betrayed everyone who loved her to get close to a man who had loved only himself?

The three of them found a booth way in the back corner of the diner. Darcy could not bear to look at her father, so she stared into her glass of soda.

"Have you heard anything from Jamee?" Hakeem asked Carl Wills.

"No. Nobody called me. Just the police. They said she ran away and asked if I knew anything. I didn't even know she was gone," he said, taking a gulp of coffee. "Do you know anything else about what happened? Did she leave a note or anything?"

"No," Darcy answered, still not looking at him. "She took all her favorite stuff and just left." *Like you did,* Darcy thought bitterly. The only difference was, everybody knew where Carl Wills had gone—to New York with that twenty-four-year-old.

"It wasn't because of me coming back, was it?" he asked again. Now, finally, Darcy looked up. She looked into the prematurely aging face of her father, at the unfamiliar ruts and crags, the scar near his left eye that had not been there five years ago. He looked as if he was in deep pain, and that was all that consoled Darcy.

"It might be that," she said. "It was a big shock to have you come back after five years. She worshiped you. You should have seen her right after you left, making up crazy lies to explain why you were still a good guy even though you'd left us. You were being held prisoner by enemy agents. You saw mobsters at the house and you left to draw them away from your family. Stuff like that. Then she learned the truth. She had all that hurt in her and now, all of a sudden, you're back, bringing all the hurt back. Maybe *that's* why she ran."

Carl Wills' hands shook as he wrapped them around the coffee cup and took several more gulps.

"She cried so much when you left, and she kept on crying because it was a wound that wouldn't heal," Darcy went on, finding comfort in his obvious misery. She wanted to somehow pile all her own pain on this man's soul, crushing him with the burden, and then be free of it herself.

Hakeem leaned over to Darcy and quietly said, "You want me to wait outside? Maybe there's something private you want to say to your father?"

"Yeah," Darcy said. Hakeem got up and left the coffee shop. A damp breeze rushed in after him, mixed with the smell of approaching rain.

"I used to wonder what I'd say if I ever saw you again," Darcy began in a flat voice. "I guess I just want to know why you did it. Left, I mean."

Darcy expected a roll call of excuses, Mom's shortcomings, his advancing middle years, his failures at his third-rate jobs, perhaps that he had been seduced by a wily young woman at a low point in his life.

"There ain't no easy answer, Darcy," Dad began, lowering his head. "I wish I could give you one, but I can't."

"You can't think of anything? Nothing at all?" Darcy asked, her voice rising. "After all these years, you have nothing to say?"

Darcy watched as her father straightened himself up in the booth. His face looked like an honest one to her for some reason, but she did not know if it was a disguise.

"Darcy," Dad went on, "I've suffered for all the suffering that I brought on you girls and your mother. You might not believe that, but it's something that

120

I've had to live with every day, and I still do. I'd do anything to be able to take back those five years, but I can't. When I left, I told myself that your mother was a strong woman with a fine job. She'd do all right without me, maybe better. Her mother was strong, too. She'd help. You girls were doing well. I told myself it was my time to be happy. And so, I left."

He took a deep breath, wiped his eyes, and continued. "Darcy, I am so sorry for the pain I caused you. Nothing I can say right now is going to take it all away. And I understand if you never forgive me. But I'm here for you. You might not believe me, but it's true. I'm here."

Darcy looked at him, unsure what to believe. She could not make her father into the noble character she once thought he was. She could not wish that fantasy man back into existence. Not all her sorrow could fix what had happened. Not all his guilt could change the past.

Darcy shoved her empty glass away and got up. She thought she heard her father mumble something about being sorry as she ran towards the door, pushed it open and fled into Hakeem's arms.

Darcy had a half-hearted hope that Jamee would be home when she got there, but she was not. Not only was there no Jamee, there was no further information on her either.

Darcy wanted the world to stop until Jamee returned. Yet she knew the next day would come just like any other. Mom's bosses expected her at work, and classes would still be held at Bluford. It all seemed like part of a cruel joke, Darcy thought.

Darcy fed Grandma some stew, and then pudding. She sat with her for a little while. Grandma said little today. She mumbled something about it being a mistake to move back to Alabama with Aunt Leticia. She said she heard wind blowing, even though there was no wind. Finally she drifted off to sleep, and Darcy went into the living room with her mother.

"I saw Dad tonight," Darcy said.

"You what?"

"He was parked across the street when I got home with Hakeem. The police called him about Jamee. He wondered if there was any news," Darcy explained.

"Did you say anything about us?" Mom asked in a shaky voice. Before Darcy could

122

answer, her mother continued. "I mean, did he ask if everything was the same?"

"No, he didn't ask, and I didn't tell him anything. I didn't tell him about Grandma being sick or anything. He doesn't deserve to know our business. He has nothing to do with us anymore," Darcy said coldly. "He looks awful, Mom. He's put on sixty pounds at least. You wouldn't know him. I'm glad he thinks he caused Jamee to run away, because he did, in a way. I'm glad he's suffering. He deserves it."

"Oh, baby, don't let the anger eat you alive," Mom cautioned.

"I asked him why he left us," Darcy said.

"I imagine he gave you an earful," Mom sighed.

"He says he's sorry and he wishes he could take the five years back. He even said he's here for me, whatever *that* means," Darcy said bitterly.

"Why, then, there's good still left in him. Only someone with good in him could feel that much guilt," Mom replied. "Don't you know, baby, truly evil people never feel guilt at all."

"It doesn't matter anymore," Darcy sighed. "I don't care what he thinks about anything. I just want my little sister home. I want Jamee home, Mom. I mean, there's so little left of our family that we can't lose another piece, don't you see?" Darcy began to cry, her tears turning into wrenching sobs. "Grandma is so sick and . . . Mom, I just want Jamee home!"

Chapter 10

Sunday was rainy and cold. The chilly wind from the night before brought in a thick dark blanket of clouds. By midday, the sky looked like doom, as if it had never been blue and would never be blue again. Darcy could not remember a time in her life when she had ever been so depressed, except for when her father had left. But even then there was anger mixed with grief. Now there was only sorrow and relentless fear. She could not find it within herself to blame Jamee for what she had done. Jamee was hurt, and in her own mind it must have seemed there was nothing to do but try to outrun the pain.

Darcy felt so helpless. She felt as if she was staring through a solid glass wall and watching her sister drown in a distant sea.

By midday the rain had stopped, and the temperature fell rapidly. Darcy shuddered at the cold, praying Jamee was somewhere warm and safe.

Mom reluctantly left for work at 3:00, instructing Darcy to call if she heard anything about Jamee. "I'll try to leave early, baby, but I'm afraid I'll lose my job if I call out sick," she explained as she went out the door.

Just after dinner, the sky began to clear, and the moon broke free of the clouds. Darcy watched it slowly rise and begin to cast its ghostly light through the window of the apartment. It had been two days since she had seen Jamee, and with each passing second, she grew more nervous.

"Jamee," Grandma called from her bedroom.

"Jamee's not here, Grandma. It's me, Darcy," she said, sitting next to her grandmother.

"Did Jamee tell you about the nice time we had in the mountains?" Grandma asked.

Darcy glanced at her grandmother.

"No, Grandma," Darcy said softly.

"Oh, what a time we had! Just the two of us. We went to the mountains and ate fried fish and listened to the wind in the trees. You should have been there. She was so happy. She laughed and laughed," Grandma recalled.

Darcy nodded, and Grandma's voice rambled on, describing adventures that had happened many years ago, as if they had happened yesterday. It gave Grandma joy to imagine happier days, so Darcy never had the heart to bring her back to reality.

"We walked to the spot where it looks like somebody just took the trees and twisted them. Jamee said maybe the moon monster did it," Grandma laughed.

Darcy glanced at her watch. It was 9:00, and there was still no word from Jamee, the police, or Mom. Frustrated, Darcy got up and helped Grandma to the bathroom and then into bed. Grandma was still smiling just before she went to sleep. "You know what Jamee said to me yesterday when we were hiking in the mountains?" Grandma asked in a confidential whisper.

"What, Grandma?" Darcy asked.

"She said, 'I'm so happy, Grandma. I'm so happy! I feel safer here than anywhere in the whole world . . . '"

After Grandma went to sleep, Darcy walked through the silent apartment. And then, suddenly, a wild thought came to her. What if Jamee had not gone downtown at all? What if she had gone to the mountains she loved so much? Maybe there was some strange truth in Grandma's dream!

Darcy ran to the phone and called Tarah. "I need a big favor. Can you and Cooper come over right away? You could stay with Grandma while Cooper drives me to the mountains. I think that's where Jamee may be."

"Sure, just hold on, girl," Tarah said.

Darcy hung up and just stared at the phone. Then, with her hands trembling, she picked up the phone and called her father.

"We're leaving for the hiking trail in the mountains to look for Jamee," she told him.

"I'll be right there," he said.

Within fifteen minutes, Cooper's pickup truck and the silver Toyota appeared. Leaving Tarah with Grandma, Darcy, her father, and Cooper headed for the mountains.

"It may just be a wild-goose chase, but Grandma was talking about the mountains just now and how Jamee was so happy there. I think maybe she'd go to the last place where she felt truly happy," Darcy explained.

"This ain't no kind of weather for a little girl to be in the mountains in jeans and a T-shirt," Cooper said ominously.

Carl Wills said nothing, but his heavy breathing hissed like the wind in the cab of the truck.

Just as they reached the mountains, a deer leaped in front of them. Cooper slowed, and the animal raced back into the woods. The Wills family had come here so many times. Darcy thought she remembered every twist and turn, but now, in the darkness, with so much time passed, it looked strange and unfamiliar. She turned to her father and asked in a frightened voice, "Do you remember where we used to hike?"

"About a half mile up this road," he said. Then, as they made a turn, he pointed, "Right there."

Cooper parked, and the three of them jumped out of the truck. The harsh cold made Darcy shiver. There were no signs of people anywhere. Not on such a night. "Jamee!" Darcy screamed, pacing around where they used to chase squirrels through the pines and cedars. The only response was the lonely cry of a coyote from the hills below.

Darcy and Cooper walked around yelling Jamee's name, but the dark, cold forest offered them only silence. Tears filled Darcy's eyes. "I was so sure we'd find her here . . ."

Carl Wills was walking around shouting with them too, but then he stopped. A strange, almost manic look entered his dark eyes. He spun around with surprising grace for such a big man and began scrambling up a nearby slope. He stumbled, dropped to his knees, got up and continued on, running, crawling. Darcy stared after him, thinking for a moment that the burden of grief and guilt had at last destroyed him, and he was running howling into the wilderness to die.

"The man don't look good," Cooper said. But before Darcy and Cooper could follow him, Carl Wills let out a loud shout. "Jamee!" And then, there he was, staggering back down the slope, the cold, wet, unconscious girl in his arms. Jamee's limp arms drooped as if she were more dead than alive.

"She was by the cedar," Darcy's father said between choking sobs. "She remembered our tree and she was huddled there. It was where I made her a princess."

Carl Wills scrambled into the front seat of the pickup with Jamee. They covered her with all their coats, and Cooper sped back down the mountain to the hospital. Jamee seemed lifeless, but she had a pulse. As she warmed, almost at the hospital, Jamee mumbled, "I got lost . . . I walked for miles, and then Grandma came . . . Grandma came, and I told her I was happier here than anywhere in the whole world."

They rushed Jamee to the emergency room where Mom worked. The doctor said another night in the cold mountains would have led to hypothermia, dangerously low body temperature, and maybe even death. When Darcy and her father were allowed to see Jamee in the small ER room, Mom was beside her. "Jamee's a lucky child," Mom sobbed, her eyes red from crying. "Praise the Lord, my baby is gonna be all right."

Darcy was alone with Jamee for a few minutes then. Mom had gone downstairs for a cup of coffee, and Carl Wills had slipped away when he knew Jamee was out of danger. "Jamee, Dad was the one who found you by the giant tree," Darcy whispered.

"Really?" Jamee's eyes filled up. "I'm sorry I ran off like I did. "I'm sorry I worried everybody."

Darcy leaned over, kissed her sister, and then joined Cooper in the waiting room. It was time to go home and let Jamee rest. In the morning Mom would bring Jamee home with her.

"I need a soda or something," Cooper said. "Let's go to the cafeteria for a second."

As Darcy walked with Cooper, she had a pang of regret about her father. She wished she had said something to him about how good it was that he had remembered just where the giant cedar was. That counted for something, didn't it? If after all this time he remembered a little thing like that, then maybe he had not put his family completely out of his heart.

As Darcy and Cooper entered the cafeteria, Darcy saw them, two people in a far corner, heads bent, talking. They both looked weary and aged beyond their years. Darcy's mother was weeping softly. When Darcy's father reached out and gently cradled Mom's cheek in his hand, Mom did not pull away. She did not smile, or embrace him, or anything like that. But she did not pull away either.

Watching them, Darcy remembered Tarah's words, "*Sometimes good people do rotten things. Then they realize the mistakes they've made and turn their lives around. . . . You can't give up on people. . . . God don't give up on us, no matter what we do. So where we get off givin' up on each other?*"

Darcy nodded and left her parents alone. Her world seemed to have shifted over the past few days. Her sister was safe, and three new loyal friends had come into her life unexpectedly when she needed them most.

Walking out into the cold darkness with Cooper, Darcy smiled to herself.

Something new was thundering in her soul—it felt like hope.

Find out what happens next at

BLUFORD HIGH

A Matter of Trust

In grade school, Darcy Wills and Brisana Meeks were friends. But all that changed at Bluford High when Darcy started hanging with "the zeros" — a group of students Brisana despises. Now the former friends are bitter rivals, and the tension between them is getting worse. For a while, Darcy tries to stay calm, ignoring her old friend's daily taunts. But when she learns that Brisana is after her boyfriend, Hakeem Randall, Darcy knows she must do something. But what?

Turn the page for a special sneak preview. . . .

Darcy was heading home when she ran into Brisana Meeks. Until just a few weeks ago, they had been best friends. When Darcy started hanging out with Tarah, Cooper and their friends, Brisana cut off the friendship. Since then, Darcy had made small efforts to repair their relationship. "Hey, Brisana," Darcy said, "how's it going?"

"Terrific," Brisana said with a sharp edge to her voice. Brisana had once told Darcy that she and Darcy were the bright, sophisticated kids at Bluford High. They were the "tens." It was their duty to avoid the low-class, stupid kids like Tarah and Cooper, who were zeroes.

"Want to go to the mall on Saturday, Brisana?" Darcy asked.

"With *you?*" Brisana scoffed, placing her hands on her hips. "No thanks," she added, leaving Darcy speechless.

As Darcy walked on, Roylin Bailey pulled up alongside her in a teal-blue Honda. "Hey Darcy, want a lift?" he shouted.

"No, thanks," Darcy said.

"Come on, Darcy," Roylin persisted. "Why are you wastin' your time with that stuttering fool? Sistah, I'm here to tell you, he ain't the one."

"Roylin, leave me alone. I don't remember asking for your opinion on my social life," Darcy snapped.

"Relax, girl. I'm just tryin' to help you out. You know, pass on the male perspective. And from where I'm sittin' you could do a lot better than Ha-ke-ke-ke-keem," he said, snickering.

Out of the corner of her eye, Darcy saw Cooper Hodden's beat-up truck roll up behind the Honda. Tarah, sitting beside Cooper, yelled, "Cooper, baby, you know your brakes ain't so good. Don't go smashin' that Honda now!"

"I can't stop!" Cooper howled, hitting the horn and blasting Roylin's Honda out of his path. Both Cooper and Tarah doubled over laughing as Roylin sped away.

"You guys are outta your minds!" Darcy said, also laughing. "Thanks, I owe you." Leaning in the truck window, she confided, "Hey, guess what. I told Hakeem I'd sign up for the talent show that's coming up, just to make him try out. Problem is, I'm terrified of getting up in front of all those people. And then there's the issue of my voice."

"What's wrong with your voice?" Cooper asked. "You talkin' okay right now."

"No, my *singing* voice. It doesn't exactly make people jump to their feet with applause. Fall to their knees begging me to stop, maybe, but not jump to their feet," Darcy said.

"Girl, don't even worry about it," Tarah advised. "Just play the music real loud, smile real pretty, and nobody'll notice how you sing."

"Thanks, I'll keep that in mind," Darcy replied sarcastically.

Darcy climbed into the cramped front seat of the pickup truck for a ride home just as Hakeem sped by on a shiny silver motorbike. Hakeem did not seem to notice Darcy, but she saw him— with Brisana Meeks sitting behind him with her arms around his waist.

"That's weird," Darcy said. "I haven't even seen his new bike, and there she is riding on it."

"He prob'ly just givin' her a lift," Tarah said.

"Don't know about that," Cooper chimed in. "That girl's *fine*."

Tarah nudged Cooper in the ribs with her elbow, and he howled. But the damage was done. It was done the minute Darcy saw Brisana riding on Hakeem's motorbike.

"Brisana always used to make fun of Hakeem because he stuttered," Darcy said.

"Stuck-up girl like her, she prob'ly just going after him to mess with your head," Tarah replied.

Or maybe, Darcy thought, *I like Hakeem a lot more than he likes me*. A cold chill pressed down on Darcy's chest like a heavy blanket of ice.